Gr

Kate Innes used to be an archaeologist and work in museums, but now she enjoys time travelling by writing historical fiction for children and adults. Kate lives in Shropshire with her family – including three big children, two greedy dogs, some nosy chickens and a visiting hedgehog.

Find out more about Kate's writing at www.kateinneswriter.com

Medieval Arrowsmith series for adults:
The Errant Hours
All the Winding World
Book 3 – out December 2021

Poetry:
Flocks of Words

Greencoats

Kate Innes

For Liz –
Who was there at
the very beginning.
Thank you for ALL
your encouragement!

Kate Innes

Mindforest Press

First published in 2021 in Great Britain by
Mindforest Press
www.kateinneswriter.com

ISBN 978-0-9934837-6-9
Copyright © Kate Innes 2021
A catalogue record for this book is available
from the British Library.

This is a work of fiction. The characters are products
of the author's imagination.

Cover and internal artwork by Anna Streetly

@magpiemateria

Cover design by MA Creative www.macreative.co.uk

For my son

John

Chapter 1

Tuesday 13ᵗʰ August, 1940
10 Hart Road, Erdington
Birmingham

A loud noise woke Gwen into complete darkness. It was a strange wailing sound, like a giant, yowling cat. Gwen sat up in bed and rubbed her eyes, trying to remember what it meant. She was reaching up to pull back the blind when her heart kicked in recognition. The air-raid siren. As she threw off the blanket, her bedroom door burst open and a thin shaft of light swept across the room, stopping at her face.

"Get up, darling! Hurry!"

It was her mother's voice. The light dipped, illuminating the floor, as she strode over to the bed and pulled Gwen to her feet. She shone the torch towards the back of the door, went to get Gwen's dressing gown and pushed it into her arms. A man was shouting outside, but Gwen couldn't make out what he was saying over the whine of the siren.

"Come on, we must get to the shelter." Her mother dragged her out of the bedroom and straight down the stairs. Gwen missed the bottom step and stumbled, knocking her chin against the blackout torch.

"Put your shoes on." Her mother steadied Gwen and pointing the torch at her old pair of shoes by the front door.

In the street, a dog, probably the Jack Russell from number fourteen, was barking frantically, adding to the relentless noise.

"Look at what you're doing!" Her mother was shoving Gwen's foot into the second shoe.

Gwen started putting on her dressing gown. There was a sick feeling in her stomach, and her chest was pounding, but there was no point saying so. Her mother had already turned away and was pulling on her own shoes and the jacket she wore to work in the rifle factory.

It looked strange over her summer nightie.

"Out the back door; you know where to go." Her mother gave her a little push. "I have to fetch Mrs Judd."

Before Gwen could say anything, she'd opened the front door and stepped out. An arc of light was sweeping across the sky, showing clouds, then black space, then clouds.

Her mother turned to close the door and saw her staring.

"Go to the shelter, now! I won't be long."

The door slammed shut. It was completely dark in the hall except for a faint glow coming from the pane of glass in the centre of the door.

Gwen put her hand on the wall to steady herself. It was vibrating. A deep rumbling was pulsing down through the bricks of the house.

Mrs Judd was the cousin of Gwen's dead grandmother, and all alone in the world, as she often complained. She would take a long time to shuffle across from number five.

Mrs Judd's next-door neighbours had offered her a space in their Anderson shelter, but the old woman had refused to go. She claimed the Brady family was 'common', and furthermore she would only shelter from the raids if 'our Lillian' escorted her.

So now Gwen's mother was putting herself in danger because Mrs Judd thought she was a better class of person than someone who drove buses in the city. And, in her first air raid, Gwen was expected to go on her own when her mother knew she hated the horrible, spider-filled shelter even in the daytime.

The rumbling was growing stronger; Gwen's hand shook with the sound. She snatched it away. There was no point waiting by the front door, trying to avoid entering the shelter alone. Her mother would bring Mrs Judd along the side passage straight to the garden. It would be better to wait by the apple tree until they arrived.

Gwen ran down the hall, through the blacked-out kitchen to the back door, feeling for the key that was always in the lock. It turned easily. She pulled the door open and stepped into the yard. The noise of engines thrummed in her chest, echoing off the terraced houses. By the low wall, the washing tub and mangle were just visible in the reflected light. Beyond that, the long, thin garden stretched into darkness.

Her father had put up the Anderson shelter just before he became poorly and had to be taken away. It was dug three feet down into the earth and crouched there like a damp, dirty toad, surrounded by beds of lettuces and potatoes. Gwen took one step towards it, stopped and looked back at the house.

What about her little brother?

She couldn't leave Hugh inside at a time like this. What would her father say if the house was bombed and there was nothing left of him?

There was a sudden cracking sound so loud that Gwen cried out, fell backwards, and sat down hard on the doorstep, her heart banging against her ribs. Overhead the arc lights were tracing a plane, and the guns were trying to bring it down. She clutched her dressing gown around her knees, staring at the stark lines of dark and light in the sky. They had explained it all at school when they'd commandeered the park to put the gun battery in place. The gunners would pick the Nazi bombers off in the sky like crows, the army captain had said.

Gwen pushed herself up and ran back into the kitchen. Hands stretched in front of her, she raced through the hall and up the stairs. All around her the sound of the firing ack-ack guns clattered off the walls.

When she reached the door of the dark bedroom, her chest was so tight it hurt to breathe. Inside was the precious photograph of Hugh taken on the beach at Rhyl the summer before he died, holding a bucket and smiling with all his new teeth. She shuffled forwards.

The special table was in the place where Hugh's cot used to be, against the inner wall. After a few steps she banged into it, and the framed photograph fell over. Her hands felt around for its edges. Then she pulled it to her chest and ran.

Gwen had reached the bottom of the stairs and was halfway down the hall when a piercing whistle directly overhead cut through the siren and the guns. It screamed towards her, louder and louder. She stumbled, dropped down and covered her ears as a wave of pressure and noise pushed her face into the floor.

Gwen wrapped her arms over her head. The hall tiles heaved and shook.

For a moment there was no air. There was no noise. Something had sucked it all away and was pressing down on her chest, crushing her.

And then all the air came rushing back, as if a dragon's hot, searing breath had roared into the house. Everything was crashing and splintering. The timbers of the stairs groaned.

Gwen didn't dare open her eyes.

The storm of noise gradually died, and all she could hear was the thudding, thudding in her chest. The rest was muffled, as if a giant cloud had descended. Thick dust was falling, making her cough. Gwen covered her mouth and raised her head.

She couldn't see anything except one beam of red-gold light through the dust. It was flickering through the hole where the glass pane in the door had been.

Gwen shook her head and her ears popped. Someone was screaming in the street, and there was the new sound of a huge, crackling fire.

Gwen pushed herself forward onto her shaking arms. The floor was strewn with broken glass. As she tried to stand, shards dropped off her back onto the floor, and her foot knocked against something hard – the photograph in its frame. Gwen picked it up and held it to her chest. Reaching out to where she thought the wall should be, her free hand snagged on a piece of splintered banister. She snatched it back and tried to wave away the clouds of dust.

Gwen started walking blindly, crunching through the glass, hand over her mouth and nose. In the kitchen, the back door was swinging open on one hinge, letting in clear air. She pushed it out of the way and went into the yard. A strange orange light was flickering on the brick wall.

"Mummy!" Gwen shouted. She ran through the gate into the garden, pulled the latch on the shelter door and half-fell inside.

"Mummy!"

The air was still and damp. There was no light – and no one.

Gwen scrambled out into the garden. The sky was so bright with flames and arc lights that she could see every leaf on the apple tree.

It was a house on Hart Road that was burning, a house at the same end as Mrs Judd's at number five.

Gwen ran into the side passage, shouting and coughing, heading for the street. She was nearly out when a large figure wearing a tin helmet appeared at the other end, blocking the light. In one hand he held a bucket.

"Get back in your shelter, m'girl!" the air raid warden shouted. "Your mam's on her way now. That's it, turn around and get in there before there's any more trouble," he said, his hard hand on her shoulder, pivoting her back towards the garden. "Go on!" She did not move, but he had already turned and was heading back down the path, blowing his whistle and signaling with his arm towards the noise and heat of the fire. "Pump this way! We need those sand buckets at the other end!"

He strode down the tile-strewn road towards two other wardens who were dragging a large, wheeled barrow piled with a hose.

"Gwen!" Her mother was limping across the street, Mrs Judd clinging to her side. "What are you doing out of the shelter? Go back – there are more planes coming!" Her mother reached the pavement and held out her free arm. Gwen ran to her, burying her face in the wool jacket, her whole body beginning to shake violently. The photograph of Hugh fell out of her hands, face up on the path.

Gwen reached down to get it, but her mother was already gathering it up. Her face looked twisted in the strange firelight.

"I've got it. Now we must go," she whispered hoarsely.

They struggled down the passage in an awkward huddle of three. Mrs Judd seemed to be unable to move of her own accord.

Eventually they emerged into the garden and got the old woman down the steps into the shelter, shutting and bracing the door behind them. It was pitch black inside. The torch must have been lost in the explosion. Gwen felt for the bench and sat down next to Mrs Judd. She was muttering the Lord's Prayer very fast, over and over.

"Matches. Where are the matches?" Gwen's mother was asking at the far end of the shelter.

All the equipment was meant to be in a watertight tin on a small table that her father had made. There was a crash as her mother knocked something over.

"Blast it!" she exclaimed, picking whatever it was up from the muddy ground. After a moment, there was a small blaze of light followed by the smell of phosphorus.

Her mother's smudged, bleeding face appeared as she put a match through the hole of a lamp and turned up the wick. She hung the lamp on a hook in the curved roof, righted the table and sat down on the bench.

"Come here, Gwennie."

Gwen slid down the bench and buried her head in her mother's lap, breathing in the smell of soap and smoke.

She felt her mother's hands in her hair, perhaps picking out splinters of wood from her plaits. Gwen couldn't hear the noise of the fire any more, or the whistling of bombs or the shouting of air raid wardens. Everything was quiet.

"Did you go back upstairs for Hugh, Gwen?" her mother whispered.

Gwen nodded into the fabric, trying not to sob. Mrs Judd hated crying children.

Her mother stroked her hair.

"You must never do anything like that ever again," she said.

Mrs Judd made a guttural sound, as if she would have said a few choice words but for all the smoke and dust caught in her throat.

Gwen squeezed her eyes shut and let out a shuddering breath.

"Which house is on fire?" she managed.

Her mother didn't answer. She had taken Gwen's clenched hand in hers.

"You're bleeding, darling."

Gwen sat up and looked at her hand. Across the palm there was a well of blood, smeared across all her fingers.

"Let me get a bandage." Gwen's mother pulled away from her and reached for the tin. She was biting her bottom lip, and Gwen could see traces of tears in the black marks on her cheeks. The blood on her mother's face was from a shallow scratch just below her hairline.

"Here, I have some water to rinse it," she said, holding out an old Thermos flask. Gwen held out her hand and they watched the reddened water fall into the earth. "It was number four," her mother said quietly as she wound a length of bandage around Gwen's hand. "A direct hit. Pray that Mrs Usher and her sister got to their shelter in time."

Mrs Judd coughed, holding her hand to her chest. It was a weak sound – raspy and dry.

"All my china is broken. The blast blew out all the windows." She looked down at her thin ankles, her feet still in slippers that were now covered in mud. "Everything is ruined," Mrs Judd said in a quavering voice. "You saw it, Lillian. The whole of the drawing room covered in plaster dust and glass." She pulled a handkerchief from the pocket of her dressing gown.

A renewed blast of firing from the guns drowned out her moans. Gwen huddled against her mother's side, shivering and looking up, although of course she could see nothing through the curved steel roof.

Her mother picked up the photograph of Hugh from the bench and held it close, her other arm around Gwen's shoulders. They sat frozen together as the guns continued their attack on the enemy planes. Mrs Judd was hunched over, her hands covering her ears.

After several minutes the guns stopped, but the quiet only lasted a few seconds before the noise and shouting from the street came back. Gwen's mother looked over at Mrs Judd. The old woman had her arms over her head, in her own world of misery, oblivious of them.

"I should have sent you with the other children. It was wrong – selfish of me to keep you here." Gwen's mother was speaking very fast and very softly, a strange fixed expression on her face. "But I wanted to believe what Mrs Judd said. I wanted to believe it was better for you to stay here rather than be evacuated and have to lodge with people who might have no manners or any idea of how to look after a child properly." She drew breath, and Gwen felt the shiver of it in her chest.

"And I didn't want to be left here alone without you, or your father." She pressed her hand to her mouth as tears trickled down her cheeks.

Gwen clung harder to her waist, but her mother quickly pulled away and straightened up, wiping her face with a crumpled hankie.

"No. It's too much. Too awful. Nowhere in Birmingham will be safe, and Alfred would never forgive me if –" She stopped mid-sentence, staring at Gwen. There was a moment of silence, and then she took a deep breath.

"Do you remember your Aunt Eglantine?"

Chapter 2

Saturday 17th August, 1940

The train struggled and panted up the steep hill. Three carriages ahead, the engine exhaled smoke and soot.

"Come away from there and sit down, Gwen. You'll get coal smuts on your blouse."

Gwen's mother was sitting in the corner of the otherwise empty compartment looking tired and anxious. She'd chosen seats furthest from the window even though the day was stifling.

Gwen sat down reluctantly and tried to brush the little black specks from her sleeves with a damp handkerchief, but this only made it worse.

It was so green outside, so different from home. Since they'd started up the hill from the station at Coalbrookdale, all she'd seen were trees. Sometimes a farm lane rutted by wagon wheels, but no houses, no shops and no people. It would be wonderful to walk through those deep, shady woods. She didn't think she'd be frightened to enter them on her own.

Her mother was fiddling with the clasp of her handbag and staring blankly at the opposite seat. On the rack above her head were their cardboard gas mask boxes and the old brown suitcase. Inside were Gwen's wool hat and gloves, four pairs of knickers, two vests, a jersey, her favourite blouse, an ugly wool skirt, a flannel, two pairs of socks, her Sunday dress and the pinafore she had worn to school. Her winter coat was in her mother's cloth bag, as it wouldn't fit.

She'd watched her mother packing the previous afternoon, perched on the end of her narrow bed. Somehow Gwen's bedroom had survived more or less intact – even the glass, which had been blown out of all the downstairs windows.

"Why are you packing my gloves and hat?" she'd asked. "It's not cold in Shropshire like the arctic, is it?"

Her mother had not looked up.

"Of course not, darling. But it will be cold in the winter, and we must be prepared for the worst. You may not be able to come home for several months."

"But I want to stay here with you," Gwen had whispered.

Her mother's eyes had remained fixed on the clothes she was placing, smooth and wrinkleless, in the case.

"Don't be difficult. You know it's too dangerous here." There'd been tears in the tremble of her voice, and Gwen had given up arguing.

Old Mrs Usher, at number four, had been killed in the blast. Her sister had escaped with her life, but nothing else. The morning after the bombing, Gwen's mother had gone straight to the post office with a letter. The next two nights more bombs had dropped on Erdington and Gravelly Hill. They'd barely slept.

On Friday when the reply from Aunt Eglantine arrived, her mother had shut herself in her bedroom. Listening at the door, Gwen heard sobbing. Her mother obviously didn't want Gwen to go to the countryside, but she wouldn't change her mind. Gwen was leaving the city, and that was that.

If she had to be evacuated, Gwen wished she could be with her school friends. But all her class had left in June and were, no doubt, having a lovely time together in South Wales. Her best friend, Annette, would come back to Erdington having become best friends with someone else. When the war was over, Gwen would probably have to sit by herself and watch them play.

The train had reached the top of the hill and was letting off steam.

"This is our stop," Gwen's mother said, patting the blond waves that curled below her hat. She'd taken extra trouble with her hair and make-up that morning, perhaps to hide the fact that she'd been crying. She stood up and swung Gwen's case down onto the seat.

"May I open the door?" Gwen asked as the train slowed and a station building came towards them.

But her mother had already opened the window and reached out to turn the handle. She was looking up and down the platform, holding tight to the door as the train lurched.

"Come now, Gwen, bring the gas masks," she said, pushing the carriage door open and stepping out gingerly with the suitcase.

Two other women and an old man were leaving the train. At the far end of the platform, a guard was talking to the driver, but otherwise the station was empty.

Gwen's stomach rumbled. It had been a long journey, and she'd gobbled the one thin cheese sandwich her mother had brought along before they'd even left the city. She very much hoped that her aunt was the kind of person who provided a good dinner.

The train moved off, and Gwen and her mother walked towards the exit. They stood on the pavement outside and looked at the quiet road. No one was waiting for them.

Her mother sighed.

"I shouldn't be surprised," she muttered.

"Does Aunt Eglantine live in this town – Much Wenlock?" Gwen asked, reading the station sign and screwing up her face against the odd name.

"No. I told you, she lives in the countryside on a little farm."

"Isn't this the countryside?"

"No," her mother said, with a slight smile. "What a city girl you are. There are shops just down that lane." She waved her left hand. A breeze caught the edge of her skirt and she smoothed it down.

"Eglantine is not very good with time keeping. If she doesn't come very soon, I will miss my train."

She looked at her small wristwatch. "It will be here in ten minutes."

A cold stone settled in Gwen's stomach.

"I thought you were staying here," she said, looking up at her imploringly. But her mother shook her head and glanced away.

"You know I have to help Mrs Judd to the shelter. What if there was another raid tonight? She won't go with anyone else."

Gwen didn't care. Mrs Judd could die in her house as far as she was concerned. She was so strict and unkind. Ever since Gwen's father had been taken to the hospital, not a day went by without Mrs Judd calling round, claiming she wanted to be helpful, while all the time demanding this and that. Gwen's mother felt obliged to help her because she was the only family Mrs Judd had left.

So Gwen was going to be left in the middle of nowhere for months and months with an aunt she barely knew, and her mother wouldn't even be there for the first night. Gwen blinked furiously and bit her lip. She was not going to cry. Not in this strange place where people would see her.

"Ah, here she is at last," her mother said, squeezing Gwen's hand.

A small cart pulled by a pony was coming down the street towards them. On the back were some milk cans, and beside the pony was a tall woman with a scarf tied over her hair. She waved as if there were a great crowd, and she must make lots of effort to get their attention. There was something moving about on the cart; it bounced up and down, in and out of view.

"Oh my goodness," said Gwen's mother. "What is she wearing?"

Aunt Eglantine was in a pair of men's overalls, patched and faded. The thing on the cart was a brown and white dog with long scruffy fur, its pink tongue lolling in the heat. They were only a few yards away now. Her aunt was grinning, and Gwen could see her wiry copper hair escaping from the headscarf. In the one photo she'd seen of Aunt Eglantine, this famous hair had still been long and plaited into two thick ropes and wound on the top of her head like a Scandinavian princess. But now it was shorn off at the neck and stood out in thick curls, more like a living mop.

Gwen looked up at her mother. She was wearing an unfamiliar expression, as if she were trying not to laugh, or cry.

The cart stopped in front of them, and the pony blew hard out of its nose like the train. Aunt Eglantine dropped the lead rein and approached her sister, giving her a kiss on the cheek. The dog had hopped off the cart and was jumping on Gwen, making dusty paw prints on her blouse and skirt, its hot breath almost reaching her face.

"Boo, get down!" Aunt Eglantine pushed the dog off her. "Go on, get back up there. No one wants your fuss in this heat!" The dog hopped back on the cart and sat panting. Gwen's aunt stood with her long legs apart and stared at her. "Goodness me, Gwen! How grown up you are already. It's only been about five years, and haven't you been shooting up behind my back?" She winked and lightly tugged one of Gwen's plaits, just like the boys did at school.

"Eglantine, try not to ruin her appearance within the first minute," Gwen's mother remarked, handing her the brown suitcase. "She only has a few clothes with her. They must be properly looked after."

"Pardon?" Aunt Eglantine said, dropping the case into the back of the cart. She looked around and furrowed her brow at Gwen, trying to work out what her sister was referring to. "Oh don't worry, I'll wash out the blouse tonight. You're in the country now," she said wagging a finger at her sister. "No one is expecting her to be spick and span. It's a good thing you won't see us splashing down the muddy farm lanes."

She turned back to Gwen.

"So, are you going to ride in the cart, young lady?"

"Yes please, Aunt Eglantine."

"No need for all that. I don't stand on ceremony. Call me Tiny. It's much less of a mouthful."

"My train will be here any moment, and I need to cross over." Gwen's mother looked at her watch again.

"Don't panic, Lil. It's usually late," Aunt Tiny said. "Here, have a sandwich." She handed a wax-paper packet to her sister who took it rather tentatively. "It won't kill you. I bake my own bread now, and nonetheless I'm as healthy as an ox!" Aunt Tiny caught Gwen's eye. "I was never known for my cooking," she confided. "Best say goodbye to your mother now, Gwen."

Gwen put both arms around her mother's thin waist.

"Don't, my darling. You'll make me cry," she said, her hand on Gwen's head. She sniffed away the sob that had been about to escape and bent down, holding Gwen at arm's length. Her eyes were full of tears. She nodded at Gwen and tried to smile.

"Be a good girl. Mind you do as you're told. I will come and see you as soon as I can. Write to me and remember your brother and father in your prayers."

Gwen clutched her mother's skirt in one hand and nodded, wanting to hide her face in the fabric.

"She must go to church on Sundays," her mother said, straightening up and detaching Gwen's hand.

"I'm sure that can be arranged," Aunt Tiny said primly, with her head on one side. "Now Gwen, you hop up on the cart, and I'll make sure your mother gets her train."

Aunt Tiny held her hand as Gwen put one foot on the ironclad wheel and clambered up. She sat down on the edge of the cart next to her suitcase. The dog came over and put its head on her lap. Little drops of saliva fell from its bright pink tongue onto the thin cotton of her skirt.

Gwen put her hand tentatively on its head. The fur was hot and soft. The dog licked her other hand, the bandaged one, and Gwen snatched it away, glancing back. Her mother often said that pets were dirty and spread diseases. Mrs Judd was of the same opinion. But her mother was climbing the railway bridge steps and talking to Aunt Eglantine. She hadn't noticed, and Gwen wouldn't have to listen to Mrs Judd for a long time. That was one good thing.

A train whistle sounded from the south, and, a moment later, she heard the rattle of wheels on the track. The dog put its paws on her lap and licked her salty face. Gwen laid her forehead on its warm fur and shut her eyes.

When she opened them again, Aunt Tiny was coming back over the bridge. The train was still idling in the station with her mother inside. Thick grey smoke rose from the funnel. A last door banged, and it moved off towards the houses and roads of the city. The dog's tail beat against the side of the cart as Aunt Tiny took hold of the pony's halter.

"I see Boo has been introducing himself in his usual way, by slobbering all over you." She looked at Gwen and raised her eyebrows. "Everything here is going to be rather like that, I'm afraid. A bit of a mess. I hope you don't mind," she smiled.

Gwen shook her head.

"Good. Hold on tight." Aunt Tiny gave the pony a gentle slap on the haunch. It turned back the way they'd come, the cart lurching sideways. "We will drop the milk cans on our way home. Just shove Boo off if he's getting too much." The dog was trying to climb onto her lap despite the sway of the cart.

"Why is he called that?" she asked, pushing his paws off her skirt and stroking his long tangled ears.

"Because he gave me a terrific shock." Aunt Tiny pulled the pony's head, and it went out into the empty main road heading north, its hooves making a loud clip-clop on the hard tarmacadam. "But a good one!" She laughed. "His full name is Bamboozle. Boo or Boozle for short."

A cloud went over the sun, and there was a chance for Gwen to look around without squinting. They were going past a row of small stone cottages. From where she sat on top of the cart, she could see into their gardens and yards, full of buckets and mangles, washing and hens.

"Did he knock you over?" Gwen asked. Whenever she stopped stroking the dog, he put his head and one paw on her lap again.

"At least a hundred times! But he got his name because he surprised me the moment he arrived." The cart was going up-hill. To the right, on an even higher slope, there was a windmill, motionless in the still, hot air. "I don't know how much you've been told, my girl. And what I should or shouldn't say."

Aunt Tiny turned around and smiled rather wickedly.

Gwen knew why she'd not seen her aunt for five years and had never stayed with her before. Aunt Eglantine had run away with an older man, a foreign painter, when she was still at art school.

She had ignored her family's advice and lived with him, here in the countryside. She'd even posed for his paintings without a stitch on. Shocking things, but they didn't seem to have made Aunt Tiny unhappy.

Gwen eyed the back of her head where the copper curls escaped the scarf. Her aunt seemed much less unhappy than her own mother, who had never done anything wrong like that.

But then Aunt Tiny had never lost a child. She didn't have any children, unless you counted the ones that the painter already had by his first wife. Three boys, all older than Gwen when her aunt and the painter married, and now grown up and gone. Gwen didn't even know their names.

The cart stopped.

On the right side of the road, a sign read 'Hill Top Farm'. The lane behind it led to some brick and timber barns. After the farm, the road dropped steeply and turned sharply, so it looked as though it disappeared. A large hill reared up in the distance beyond the patches of woods and fields.

Boo jumped down and started sniffing around the sign, lifting his leg, as Aunt Tiny came round the back of the cart.

"Bring the cans over here, Gwen."

They were lighter than they looked. Gwen shuffled them to the back of the cart, and tall Aunt Tiny lifted them by the handles one at a time and put them down next to the sign. Behind the farm buildings, a flight of large black birds rose from a strip of forest on the ridge and flew over them towards the valley. The sight of their wide, dark wings gave Gwen a shiver of excitement.

"You'd best walk this bit," Aunt Tiny said, taking the pony's rein again, "or the cart will overtake the horse on the steep hill."

As Gwen climbed down, the hem of her skirt caught on a jutting nail. She looked down in dismay. It was one of only two skirts she had brought with her. If she had torn it on her first day, within the very first hour, what would her mother say?

She pulled the thin cotton round to look. It was not so bad. The thread had pulled loose, but the fabric had not torn.

Her aunt was tugging the reluctant pony back towards the road and didn't seem to have noticed. With a needle and thread, Gwen could hem it again before tomorrow, and her mother need never know. She smoothed the skirt down and ran a little to catch up with Aunt Tiny, falling into step with her.

"Mummy told me that you married Mr Høeg, but none of the family liked him," Gwen said, hoping this would be enough to get her aunt talking again.

"That is what I would call a glorious understatement," Aunt Tiny said, kicking a loose stone with her boot.

They were winding down the gradient of the hill, trying to slow the momentum of the wheels by making the pony go side to side.

"Yes, I married Mr Høeg, but I always called him Anders, so you can too. He was an artist, and so am I." She looked up at the bright, cloud-flecked sky and wiped the sweat from her forehead. "My family didn't like him for many reasons, but we don't need to think about that. He was a good man, and I was very sad when he died in the winter almost two years ago. It was a sudden thing. He was chopping wood, and he had a heart attack. He only lived a few minutes, but I was there when he died, thank God."

Gwen dropped her gaze. Her aunt seemed so strong and jolly; she didn't want to see her upset.

"A month later, I was chopping wood in exactly the same place," Aunt Tiny continued, sounding quite calm. "I must say I was crying a little, which is not a good thing when you are using an axe. Please take note," she said, nodding at Gwen. "I missed the log, and it flew off the stump and hit me in the shin. It was so sore, it started me crying even harder."

She looked behind at Boo who was still riding on the cart. He wagged his tail and licked his muzzle. Aunt Tiny smiled.

"I was sitting on the ground, holding my leg and crying like a baby, not understanding how lucky I was that I hadn't hit my leg with the blooming axe, and the next thing I know, I'm being licked all over by this boy." She waved her hand at the dog. "Never seen him before in my life. No collar. Half-starved. Wouldn't leave me alone."

Aunt Tiny looked down and took Gwen's hand. "You may think this is strange, and no doubt it is, but I am sure that Anders sent that dog to be with me because he couldn't comfort me himself. So, now that Boozle is living with me, and he is just as messy and demanding as Anders was, I don't feel so alone."

She gave Gwen's hand a brisk shake and began swinging it forwards and back.

"There it is, and now you can believe all the things they told you about me are true. I am a crazy aunt!"

Gwen giggled.

"They didn't say that."

"I bet they did. And worse!"

Gwen looked up at her. She was grinning her wide smile. Not sad, not crying.

"Well, a few things."

"I'm lucky they let you come. Such a bad influence."

"Mrs Judd thinks you should come home to Birmingham now that Mr Høeg – sorry, Anders – is dead."

Aunt Tiny sucked air through her teeth like a whistle.

"Does she?"

"And mother thinks you should find a nice man your own age to marry," Gwen said before she could stop herself.

"Well I never!"

Suddenly Aunt Tiny turned to look straight at Gwen.

"Young lady, have you been eavesdropping?"

Gwen lowered her head. She had said the wrong thing, gone too far. But Aunt Tiny squeezed her hand tight in her calloused one.

"I would expect nothing less. I used to be a champion eavesdropper in my day. Heard so many secrets it made my hair curl!"

Gwen snorted a laugh of surprised relief.

Aunt Tiny tugged on the pony's mane, and it stopped at a gate on the left. The sign read 'Netherwood'.

"Here we are."

It was a strange, ramshackle house. On the ground floor the rough wooden beams showed on the outside, and the bricks between them were old and cracked. Everything was at an angle. Even the upper floors had windows that seemed wonky and squashed.

Attached to the main house was a brick pantry, and, alongside that, another smaller lean-to. The house looked as if it had been reproducing smaller versions of itself for some time.

They took the pony and cart past the house to a stable at the far end of the yard. An open shelter stood next to it. Logs were stacked to one side, and, in the middle, there was a large axe lodged in a chopping block.

Aunt Tiny was unharnessing the pony. She had just removed the collar when she saw Gwen staring at the block. For the first time, her face wrinkled with worry. Slowly she hung the collar on a hook. When she turned back, her expression was calm again.

"It may take a bit of getting used to, but you must try not to mind. Anders did die right there, but his body is buried in the churchyard where it should be." She tethered the pony loosely to the stall, and it started to drink from a bucket. "Now, let's get some lunch. I could eat that horse!"

They had bread and cheese, small bright red tomatoes, and a handful of lettuce in which Gwen found a tiny slug. She pushed the leaf to the back of her plate and took a sip from her glass. The water tasted stony and hard. The long kitchen table was made of dark wood, scratched and very old. In the middle was a bunch of flowers in a blue jug. A bee was working its way from flower to flower. Aunt Tiny watched it, her mouth full of bread.

"It's going to be a good year for honey," she said after swallowing. The bee took off towards the small paned window and bashed against it. Aunt Tiny got up, lifted the widow latch and wafted the bee outside. "I will show you around when you've finished. And then I expect you'd like some time to settle in." Aunt Tiny stood with the light of the window behind her. She pushed her headscarf off and gave her head a shake. Her hair stood out like a burnished halo.

"There are very few rules in this house. But the most serious one is this: every afternoon I work for several hours, and it is very important that I can concentrate. So you can either go out or stay in, but near my studio," Aunt Tiny pointed outside to a low building with large windows, "you must be as quiet as a mouse."

Aunt Eglantine's work was another thing Gwen had heard bad things about. It was not the kind of art a woman should be making, apparently. Metal sculptures. Some of them wearing no clothes. Gwen would like to see them, but she probably wouldn't be allowed.

"Yes, Aunt." She wiped her mouth with the striped napkin and stood up. "Thank you for dinner. I mean lunch."

Aunt Tiny laughed.

"You sound like a little soldier. Manners are simply super but only in small doses. As long as you clear up after yourself, don't mind about the rest." She scratched her head and then tied the scarf on tightly. "Right, let's start at the top of the house – your bedroom."

They went up two flights of very uneven stairs and came to a small landing. Two low, white doors stood on opposite sides.

"That is just a storeroom. You can look in if you want," Aunt Tiny said, pointing to the one on the right. "All the boys' old books and toys are in there, but it hasn't been dusted in years. This is your room." And she opened the left-hand door.

Chapter 3

The room had low, sloping, beamed walls. There was one window. The rolled-up blackout blind was leaning against its sill. Opposite was a brass bed with a bright blue bedspread. The floorboards were covered with a patterned carpet like the ones in picture books of oriental palaces. Someone had glued scraps of newspaper and pictures of planes and cars on the beams. A washstand stood to one side of the window, a small table and chair on the other. And best of all, next to the bed was a tiny fireplace, laid with sticks.

Gwen looked down at the intricate carpet.

"Do you think you will be comfortable? I am only down one flight of stairs. I'm sure I'll hear you if you call, or you could always bang on the floorboards!" Aunt Tiny pulled back the faded curtains further. "You can see so far from up here."

She yanked open the window.

"Anders used to paint in this room after the boys left home. He loved the way the weather changed the view every minute of the day. That's why I put this great big carpet down, to cover all the paint spatters."

"It's beautiful," Gwen said.

From the window she could see the pony by its stall, now grazing on the tufts of grass growing amidst the cobbles, the chickens scratching the ground around their pen, and then, beyond that, a wood where birds were calling and alighting.

"Good." Aunt Tiny clapped her hands, turned her back on the window and crossed the room in three strides. "Let's see the rest of the house. It's nearly time for me to start work."

There were three other bedrooms. As she'd said, Aunt Tiny's was just below Gwen's, its window also looking south. Almost every inch of the walls seemed to be covered in a painting or a sketch, finished or not, some framed, some torn from a notebook.

Aunt Tiny opened the other two doors opposite hers, but didn't go in. They were small, nearly identical rooms, containing only a bed, a wardrobe and a wooden chair.

"Lawrence and Peter, the older boys, use these rooms. They don't often visit, but when they do, they spend all their time eating or roaring around outside," Aunt Tiny said cheerfully. "So there's no point wasting good furniture on them. You have John's room. If all three visit while you are here, which is an almost unheard-of privilege, they can bunk up together."

On the ground floor, Aunt Tiny led her into a large room with an empty easel by the window. Dried paint marked the floor.

"This was Anders' studio, and it is not a room to play in. It must stay just as it is. I'm sure you understand."

Aunt Tiny did not look at Gwen when she spoke. She was standing very still with one long finger resting on the easel.

"Yes, Aunt."

"I suppose that is another rule. I didn't think there would be more than one. But that's better than one thousand, I believe." She turned around, her lips pressed together. Then she sighed. "Now, please stop calling me 'Aunt'. It sounds too frightful. Why don't you call me 'Auntie' or 'Tiny'. But not both. Come and see the parlour."

The parlour was dark, and when Aunt Tiny opened the thick velvet curtains, dust rose in waves through the sudden sunshine. There was a very old settee, two sunken chairs and an upright piano. Gwen went over to it. The sheet of music on the stand was puckered and faded. The title was 'Let me call you Sweetheart'.

"Do you play?" her aunt asked, wiping the dust from the top of the piano with a fingertip.

"No, but Daddy does. I usually sing when he plays."

"Ah. You must miss that," Aunt Tiny said. "Maybe you will sing while I play sometime?" She touched Gwen's shoulder lightly and pushed the door open with her toe. "Now let's go outside."

They crossed the sunlit yard, heading towards the chickens and the vegetable garden.

"I think you are old enough to do some jobs, Gwen?" Aunt Tiny said, picking up a garden fork that was lying on the grass.

Gwen nodded.

"As you can imagine, I've been doing everything on my own for a while, so you can decide what you want to do. No point doing something you hate." She stopped a moment and fixed Gwen with her green eyes. "But choose wisely, because whatever you do I will stop doing. If you forget, it won't get done. I don't have time for chasing people. Anders' sons had the same choice. I will show you what they used to do, and you can decide."

In the end Gwen chose to brush the pony, whose name was Hilda, feed the chickens and collect the eggs.

"Sometimes you need to be a detective to find them all," Aunt Tiny warned. "One of the hens thinks she's an acrobat, laying eggs in the most mind-boggling places. I've done that chore today, but Hilda will need brushing before tea."

"What's down there?" Gwen pointed beyond the chicken pen and the studio to the line of dark trees.

"That is our wood – Netherwood Coppice. It's yours to explore. There is a stream too, down the hill. But before that, I should also show you our shelter. Not that we ever hear the air-raid siren, but they said we had to build one, so I did."

Aunt Tiny led her over to a low shack between two trees.

It was more like a lean-to than a proper shelter, stocked with a few tins and blankets wrapped in oilcloth, as well as a camp bed and an old chair.

A chicken had laid an egg in the saucepan on the camp stove. Aunt Tiny gave it to Gwen.

"Here, your first bit of treasure. Take it to the kitchen. Boil it if you are hungry this afternoon. Tea won't be until after seven."

And she strode off towards her studio.

It was hard to resist running straight into the wood, but her mother's voice spoke in her mind, and Gwen went back to the house to change into her play clothes. Having no friends wouldn't be too bad with so much land to explore, but the shelter would have been a wonderful den for her and Annette. They'd made one at the very back of Gwen's garden, in a patch of waste ground by an old compost heap, but Mrs Judd had shouted at them that it was a dirty place to play, and they'd had to go inside.

Gwen went through the kitchen and began climbing the stairs. Halfway up she stopped. A shaft of sunlight was illuminating a painting on the wall. Gwen peered at it curiously. At first it seemed to be an ordinary picture of a forest at sunset, but as her eyes adjusted to the gloomy foreground, she saw strange wooden creatures emerging from the trunks of the trees. They had eyes and mouths, and their hair and hands were sprouting twigs. Some were elegant and young, others wizened and weathered, but all were formed of branches and leaves. Something about the brushstrokes made the creatures look as if they were coming out of the painting, fixing her with their questioning eyes.

A shiver went down Gwen's back, as if one of those twiggy fingers had traced her spine. Although they were small, it was hard to stop looking at the creatures. She had the strangest feeling that their mouths were about to open, that they had something to tell her. One of the largest stood beneath a huge oak. Nearby, a much smaller figure was leaning against a holly trunk, the red berry of its nose made with the lightest touch of a brush.

Gwen shook her head, and the creatures swam out of focus. She peered at the painting again, looking for a signature, but there were only the initials 'A H' on the bottom right. Anders Høeg, she guessed. Were these trees part of Netherwood Coppice? When she went into the woods, she would have to look out for the big oak.

Gwen dragged her eyes away from the painting, ran up to her room and opened her case. She found her old wool skirt and brown socks, and, after putting them on, pulled off the fresh bandage that her mother had put on early that morning. The cut was almost healed but was very itchy where the scab had formed. Gwen examined it and gave it a scratch. Her father would surely have declared that 'it needed some air'.

Gwen shut the door and clattered down the stairs. Boo was drinking from a bowl outside the door. He looked up, dripping water from his shaggy muzzle.

"Are you coming with me?" Gwen said, walking away and holding out her hand. He ran over and nuzzled her palm, making it wet and slimy. She wiped it on the grass and set off across the small field towards the wood, the dog at her heels.

She found the stream quickly. At least Boo found it, and she found him. He was running in and out of the shallows, soaking wet and muddy already. In the patches of sun, the drops of water flying from his fur looked like sparks of light.

Gwen took off her shoes and socks and waded in. It was only up to her shins but very cold. There were lots of sticks to make a dam, but Boo didn't understand what she was doing. He kept taking them away and chewing them to shreds.

The sun had dropped out of view by the time Gwen sat down on the footbridge to pull socks onto her wet, puckered feet. She was just tying her shoelaces when the sound of whistling made her turn, startled.

A boy was coming down the path from the other side of the wood. He was dark-haired, quite tall and, because he was looking down, hadn't seen her yet. If she was quick, she could get away without having to talk to him. It would be so embarrassing to try to explain who she was and why she was there.

"Come on, Boo," she called, nearly tripping in her hurry to get off the bridge, "it's late." Behind her the whistling stopped. He would be watching her, would be just about to shout. Gwen grabbed Boo's collar and ran up the steep path towards Netherwood, keeping her eyes fixed on the dog bouncing at her side.

She didn't look back to see if the boy was following until she'd reached the field by the house. Behind her, in the dark trees, the only whistling sound was birdsong.

Hopefully he wouldn't turn up there again. She didn't want to have to share the stream with an annoying boy. It was her aunt's land, after all.

"Good dog." Gwen patted Boo's head. He barked once and raced off towards Aunt Tiny's studio. She followed slowly, getting her breath back.

Beyond the house, the low sunlight glowed on the high ridge of trees she'd seen when they stopped at the farm. The same black birds were circling above it in the warm evening air. It was not far away. From there, she might even be able to see Birmingham, but not at night, when the blackout made the city disappear. Gwen hated having to tape the windows shut. It was like living in a dark, sealed box, waiting for a giant to take off the lid.

She shivered, remembering the smoking rubble of Mrs Usher's house, and forced her thoughts back to the yard and her chores. Hilda was standing quietly in her stall. Presumably brushing a pony was a combination of brushing one's hair and sweeping the floor. By the time she'd finished, maybe Aunt Tiny would have come out of her studio and started cooking.

The pony was very patient with her lack of experience, but at one point she did try to bite Gwen's plait when it fell across her nose. And just as she was about to brush her tail, Hilda did a large dropping. It nearly landed on Gwen's foot. She was hot and tired when she finished, and not quite as pleased with her choice of jobs as before.

Compared with the farmyard sounds outside, the kitchen was dark and quiet. A clock was ticking. It seemed unnaturally loud in the still house. She went to find it. The hands pointed to half past seven. Where had all the hours gone? The wood and stream had consumed the whole afternoon. Gwen yawned. She had been up since six in the morning to get on the first train. Her empty stomach was complaining, but there was no sign of Aunt Tiny. It seemed she would have to boil the egg after all and eat by herself.

Gwen had just climbed on a chair to reach for a saucepan hanging on a hook above the cooker when the door scraped on the flagstones, and she nearly fell.

The dog rushed in followed by Aunt Tiny who was taking off a very stained apron.

"There you are," she said, rubbing her forehead and leaving a smear of clay on her face. "You look just as muddy as me. What a good thing your mother isn't here to see us!"

Gwen was so tired she nearly fell asleep in her omelette and toast. Aunt Tiny insisted that she wash the mud off her legs before going to bed and gave her a basin of warm water. Once under the covers, Gwen only saw the strange darkness of her sloping bedroom walls for a moment before her eyes shut, and she fell asleep.

But almost immediately it seemed that she was surrounded by a deep throbbing noise. In her dream it was a huge lion, its purr turning into a threatening rumble. She lay as still as possible, her heart racing. The whole room trembled as the noise got louder.

Gwen ran to the window, pulled back the blind and stood looking out. The moon was nearly full and below it was a bright star that became bigger and bigger.

A plane was coming. It was over the wood, over the house and past them, and then there was a hand on her shoulder.

"Gwen, Gwen, stop shouting! Come back to bed. They are all gone."

Aunt Tiny was in a long white nightgown. She looked like a ghost with black shadows under her eyes. Gwen's mouth was dry, her throat sore. She'd been screaming something at the planes.

"What?" she whispered, following Aunt Tiny to the bed. "What was I saying?"

Her aunt pulled the cotton blanket up and smoothed it down across Gwen's shoulders. Her face was just a pale smudge in the darkness.

"You were saying 'Go away – you can't have my brother.'" Aunt Tiny felt her forehead with the back of her hand. "You must have had a dream about poor Hugh, and the planes woke you up."

Gwen felt tears sliding down her face onto the pillow.

"A lion ate him," she sobbed.

There was a long silence. Aunt Tiny was stroking her hand.

"That's a horrible dream, but it's over now."

Gwen tried to stop crying. She shouldn't be so silly on her first night at her aunt's – screaming and waking her up.

Her mother had told her that planes might fly over Shropshire, but it was nothing to worry about. They only dropped bombs on factories or cities, so there was no reason for Gwen to be afraid. If Aunt Tiny told her mother about this, she'd be cross that Gwen had caused so much trouble.

As her breathing slowed down, she thought she could still hear the rumble of planes.

"Do they come every night?"

"No. This is only the second time. The ones that fly over us are heading north, maybe to Liverpool. But it is very good you are here, where it's safe."

Gwen screwed her eyes shut. There were probably other planes flying to Birmingham, preparing to drop more bombs on Hare Road. Her mother could be killed in her bed, and so could Mrs Judd. Gwen didn't really want her to die. God must listen to her prayers and stop the planes.

"I'll let you get back to sleep, Gwen," Aunt Tiny was saying. "You'll be so tired."

Gwen nodded, not opening her eyes. It was important not to be any trouble, but her dreams were beyond her control. So she must stay awake, at least until the planes had returned.

As soon as she heard Aunt Tiny shut her bedroom door downstairs, Gwen crept out of bed and went back to the window.

A few ragged clouds were dimming the moonlight. Further out, there were bright clusters of stars, but she didn't know the names of the constellations. The only one her father had taught her was The Plough, and she couldn't see that anywhere. Perhaps it was visible from wherever he was. Perhaps he was looking at it tonight and thinking of her. But her mother had said that his mind was so crowded with grief, and with all the bad things that happened to him in the first war in France, that he couldn't think of either of them at the moment. There was no room.

Gwen wiped her eyes with the sleeve of her nightie and looked down at the moonlit yard. There was the bucket by the pony's stall, the cart tipped on its end, and the henhouse. Beyond the relative brightness of the field, there was the deeper darkness of the wood. She put her elbows on the sill and rested her head on her arms. The wood was lovely in the day, but she wouldn't want to go there at night. There would be foxes at the very least. Of course the strange wooden creatures from the painting on the stairs wouldn't be there. They looked like the illustrations in her book of Fairy Tales. And lions lived in Africa, not England, as everyone knows.

Something moving in the meadow caught her eye. A low, broad animal was pushing through the grass, coming towards the house. Gwen longed to jump into bed and hide under the covers, but she gripped the edge of the window and shook her head.

She would not go back to bed until the planes had definitely gone for good.

Gwen looked out again. The animal took a while to find as it had moved surprisingly quickly across the meadow. As it lifted its head, she saw a white stripe and a long snout. A badger. Nothing worse. It put its head down into the grass again, looking for food. She watched it waddle right up to the chicken pen where it stretched its muzzle and held still for a moment, then turned tail and headed across the meadow like a tugboat on the sea. Soon Gwen heard it too – the familiar rumble of planes.

There were eight. She sat watching them disappear into the clouds and stars, wanting to reach out and tear them from the sky. But that was pointless. They'd dropped their bombs on Liverpool already; the damage was done. Gwen felt her way to the bed and pulled the blanket over her head. She couldn't stop shivering.

If only her mother had let her bring Hugh's teddy. But there wasn't room in the suitcase, and really wasn't she too old for toys like that? Gwen pulled the pillow over her head as well. If she had another nightmare, perhaps it would stifle her cries.

Chapter 4

Gwen woke up to a smelly tongue licking her face. She had moved in the night, and the pillow was on the floor. Boo was standing on it with his dirty paws. He barked happily at her.

"Hello," Gwen said, reaching out her hand. He licked that too.

She got out of bed and went to the window, lifting off the blackout blind. The sun was already quite high in the sky. Aunt Tiny was in the yard, feeding the pony.

The hens would be hungry. There would be no eggs for breakfast if she didn't do her job. Boo nosed her hand as she went to get dressed.

"What do you want, boy? Are you hungry too?"

He just sat watching her as she changed into her old clothes. It was rather unnerving. But as soon as she was finished, he raced down the stairs ahead of her.

Gwen stood in the kitchen, unsure whether to help herself to the milk in the jug and the bread on the board. She went to the door and looked out. Aunt Tiny was striding towards her, carrying a bunch of dirty carrots by their green tops. Gwen moved aside to let her through the doorway.

"Good morning, Auntie."

Gwen kept her eyes lowered, hoping Aunt Tiny wouldn't mention the planes or her shouting in the night.

"Hello Gwen," she said, dumping the carrots in the sink in the pantry. "It's a beautiful morning. Help yourself to breakfast. There is some jam somewhere. Ah there it is." She reached it down from a shelf on the far wall. "Butter is in that pot." She pointed to a covered earthenware dish.

"You don't mind eating by yourself, do you? Well, you won't be by yourself because Boo is at every meal. I must weed out the leeks before the sun is too hot." And she was gone again.

Gwen sat down with two slices of bread, made herself a jam sandwich and poured a cup of milk. It was remarkable how different her mother and her aunt were. What made her mother so careful and serious and Aunt Tiny so lighthearted and indifferent to rules?

The plum jam was very good. Gwen wondered if she was allowed another sandwich and decided she was. She couldn't imagine her aunt caring if she ate in an unladylike way, so she gobbled it and wiped her mouth on the back of her hand. It wouldn't matter; she was only going to see the chickens and her aunt, neither of whom cared what she looked like. Gwen went to the door, clicking her sticky fingers for the dog to follow.

But in the yard, standing in front of her aunt and holding a basket, was a boy, tall and black haired – the boy who'd been at the stream. Gwen tried to disappear back into the kitchen, but her aunt had seen her.

"Gwen, come and meet my friend."

She walked slowly over to them. The boy looked just as embarrassed as she felt.

"Gwen this is Edward, Eddie for short. And Eddie, this is Gwen, my niece from Birmingham." Aunt Tiny grinned at them. "Eddie has brought me some rashers of bacon and some sausages from their farm. He lives this side of Wigwig."

Gwen giggled at the name, then put her hand over her mouth. Eddie glanced at her disapprovingly.

"Eddie, I'd be grateful if you would take this money back to your mother, and please tell her I now have a visitor staying and need twice the ration. Gwen, go with him and introduce yourself to Mrs Jones. Then bring the bacon and sausage back with you."

Aunt Tiny was holding out a coin, which Eddie pocketed.

"But I haven't done the chickens yet, Auntie," Gwen said, horrified.

"Don't worry," she said, waving her long and dusty hand at them and heading back towards the vegetable beds. "Eddie will help you do it before you go."

They stood watching her as she strode away. Gwen twisted her finger around the hem of her skirt, hoping he wouldn't mention her running away the previous evening.

Eddie put his hands in the pockets of his grubby waistcoat and cleared his throat.

"Well. Let's get your job done. I don't want to be late back," he said, trying to sound like a grown-up. He probably was older than her, but not by much.

He was tall but also thin, and there was no trace of hair on his lip.

They filled the feeders and collected the eggs in silence. There were too many to hold in their hands, so Gwen held out her skirt and they filled it up. It felt strange walking with the eggs moving around. If they broke, they'd make an awful mess. She stepped carefully towards the kitchen.

"Ha, you look like you are doing a huge egg and spoon race," Eddie laughed.

"Well, you aren't helping. You need to lift them out and put them in the basket."

"You should have taken the basket with you, silly," Eddie said, taking them out of her skirt four at a time and placing them carefully in the basket on the kitchen dresser.

"I would like to see you in Birmingham at this time of day with all the trams and buses going by. You might not be such a know-it-all then," she retorted.

The eggs were all stowed, and Gwen shook out her skirt.

"All right, no need to get cross." He headed for the door. "Come on, we have to go or I'll be late."

"Late for what?"

"Just late. I've got jobs to do."

"Do you live on a farm like this?"

"Ha," he huffed. "This is no farm. We have eighteen cows and twenty pigs. Also nearly fifty sheep."

Gwen kept quiet and dropped back a little.

He turned to look at her and licked his lips as if he were nervous.

"But your aunt has a nice place here. It's good land. Lots of wood. I bet she could keep pigs in the forest like they did in the old days if she wanted to."

"I saw a badger here last night," Gwen said. They were just reaching the edge of the wood to join the path down to the stream. "He came out of the woods just over there."

"That's where their sett will be," Eddie picked up a fallen stick and slashed at the tall grass. "There'll be young ones at this time of year. You might hear them at night. They come out and play around the entrance to their den. If they were on my father's land, he would set his dogs on them."

"That's horrible," Gwen cried.

Eddie shook his head.

"In the countryside, pests have to be kept under control," he said importantly.

"You don't know about farming, but I bet you'll like eating our bacon and sausages."

She didn't answer. She was glad the badger she'd seen was on her aunt's land. Eddie was either showing off, or he really was horrible. Either way she wasn't going to tell him about what she saw any more. She trudged after him, her lips pressed shut.

Eddie went down the slope towards the stream. The day before Gwen had gone no further, finding plenty to do in the shallow pools and small waterfalls. She'd stood on the narrow footbridge and thrown sticks in like a little girl. But then there'd been no one to see her.

"How did you get here?" Eddie glanced at her out of the corner of his eye. "Does your father have a car?"

"No. I came on the train. We're not rich."

"I thought everyone in cities had cars. They're thick with them, aren't they?"

"No, it's mainly trams and buses."

"Oh."

He fell silent again. They were coming out on the other side of the wood into a sloping meadow. Sheep were grazing by the stile. Eddie clapped his hands, and they startled and trotted away.

"Mind where you put your feet. The cows were in here last week and there will be a few pats left behind."

"I'm not blind," Gwen muttered under her breath.

"What does your father do?" Eddie asked, stopping halfway up the hill. He was obviously trying hard to make up for what he'd said about the badgers. But that was a difficult question to answer.

"He's a pharmacist."

"A what?"

"A pharmacist. A chemist. You know, a man who dispenses medicine."

"Oh, right. He must be pretty rich then. Medicines cost a fortune."

"Well, he isn't. He doesn't get all the money. He has to buy the medicines in. And besides he is not very well, so he can't work at the moment."

"What's wrong with him?"

Gwen began striding up the hill, her head down. If only Eddie would stop asking questions.

"Let's just go and get the blooming sausages. It's too hot." She felt her face burning with shame.

He caught up with her quickly on his long legs.

"Sorry," he mumbled.

"It's all right," she muttered back.

"Hey, look. Your crazy dog is coming with us!" He pointed down the hill where Boo was just clearing the stile.

"He's not my dog." But Gwen couldn't stop herself from smiling as Boo came lolloping towards her.

"Your aunt's then. But he is crazy."

"He's very clever," Gwen claimed, stroking his ears and turning her face away from his tongue. "Very clever people are often considered crazy, and it's the same with dogs."

"That makes sense." Eddie grinned.

"How old are you?" Gwen asked, grabbing a long stalk of grass as she walked and putting it in her mouth to match Eddie's. She chewed the end before spitting it out.

Eddie took the stalk out of his mouth and blew an imaginary smoke ring.

"Old enough to have tried a real cigarette," he bragged.

"No you're not."

"I've got two older brothers. They gave me one. It was horrible," he admitted. "I'm nearly twelve. My eldest brother is in France."

"Oh."

Gwen felt deflated. He wouldn't be in the same class as her at school. She'd know no one and have to start from scratch.

"He'll be fine though. Harry knows how to look after himself," Eddie said with a swagger. "He's with lots of his mates. They all joined up together in the SRLI."

Gwen guessed that must be a local regiment.

"Has he come home since?"

"Yeah, in the summer. After Dunkirk."

He fell silent. No one wanted to talk about the retreat across the Channel from Dunkirk.

After a moment they reached a lane, and Eddie turned right.

"It's not far now."

They started down the road, the sun directly above them and Boo trotting at their heels.

"Have you ever seen a fossil?" Eddie asked.

Gwen looked over at him.

"That's a funny question." She paused. "Do you mean the animals that turned into stone, like dinosaurs? I've seen some of them in a museum."

"Could you touch them though?"

"No, they're in glass cases, of course."

"Well, I can show you where you can find your own fossils. To keep," Eddie said, looking up at the sky as if the fossils were falling from it like rain.

Gwen snorted.

"You don't believe me?"

"I didn't say that."

"I'll show you tomorrow, if you like."

"All right then," Gwen said.

"Bring some food with you. It's a climb," Eddie said. "Here's the farm."

As it happened, Eddie's mother was as preoccupied as Gwen's aunt. She was making pies in the large farmhouse kitchen. They smelt wonderful. Mrs Jones looked up and nodded at Gwen as Eddie introduced her. She wiped her hands on her apron, counted out Gwen's change from a jar on the shelf, and went to wrap up the sausages and bacon.

"There we are." She handed the packet to Gwen. "Spect I'll see you again." And she went back to her work.

Eddie led Gwen outside again into the crowded yard. An old tractor was parked by one of the barns. Near it Boo and one of the farm dogs were sniffing each other. Several geese were approaching, hissing.

"You best go. Those geese are vicious," Eddie said, waving his arms. "I wouldn't fancy your dog's chances. I'll come and get you tomorrow when I've finished my jobs."

Boo started barking loudly as the geese trapped him against the brick pigpen.

"Here, I'll distract them." Eddie rushed at the geese and they scattered. "Get going."

He pushed Gwen and Boo out of the gate. The geese were honking loudly and flapping their great white wings.

"Goodbye,' Gwen called, but the noise of the geese drowned her out, and Eddie had already disappeared from view.

Gwen was thinking of so many things, fossils and geese, dogs and soldiers, that she nearly missed the turning onto the footpath from the meadow. She stopped on the bridge, and Boo sat down in the water, lapping it up.

Then he bounded out, shook himself and jumped up to sniff the packet of meat.

"No, Boo," she shouted.

She found him a stick instead and threw it in the stream for him to fetch. He didn't tire of the game.

"Are you sure you are so clever?" she asked him, hiding the stick and watching him look forlornly for it. She called Boo over, and they climbed the slope up towards the house.

Chapter 5

That evening Gwen was just as tired as before, thanks to her disrupted night. It was hard to concentrate on what Aunt Tiny was saying as they washed and dried the dishes together.

"Off you go to bed," her aunt said, seeing Gwen yawn for the fifth time. "This fresh country air is catching up with you. You'll sleep like a log tonight."

That prediction turned out to be correct. Whether she slept through the planes or they didn't come at all, Gwen had a long uneventful night and only woke to the clock striking downstairs. She counted seven, but she may have missed one.

She went to the window and removed the blind. It was raining. That would probably mean no trip to find fossils; she'd be stuck inside all day. Her aunt was in the vegetable patch, her hair covered by a wide oilcloth hat. The pony was hiding in her stable. The rain beat loudly against the windowpane in a sudden gust of wind. Her aunt straightened up, threw some weeds over her shoulder and ran for the house.

Gwen washed her face and dressed quickly. She could hear her aunt in the kitchen, whistling and talking to the dog, and she didn't want to miss her.

"Good morning," Aunt Tiny said. She was drying her hands on a tea towel. Water was still dripping from her hair. The hat hung on the back of the door and was making a substantial puddle on the floor. "Nice weather for mermaids. I got rather cold out there. Would you like a cup of tea?" The kettle was just coming to a boil.

"Yes please."

"Make your own toast." Her aunt spooned tea leaves into a pot.

"Will it rain all day?" Gwen asked, finding the bread knife and trying to keep the cut straight.

"I shouldn't think so. 'Rain before seven, dry by eleven' they say. Give it an hour on either side, and I'd say that it will be fine this afternoon." She poured out the steaming water. "It does make the chickens very sorry for themselves," she chuckled "and it's too wet for a part-time gardener like me. I'm going to write a letter to your mother instead. What about you? There are some good books in the attic when you've finished your jobs."

Gwen decided not to ask Aunt Tiny if she'd heard anything on the wireless about the air raid the first night. Her aunt appeared open and friendly, but it was clear there were things she didn't want to talk about. The war was one. She acted as if it was a minor irritation and best ignored. But Aunt Tiny was writing to Gwen's mother, and presumably that meant that their house had not been bombed, or how could the letter be delivered?

Aunt Tiny was right about the chickens; they made mournful noises at her as she moved among them to find the eggs. She was also right about the books. There were lots and lots, piled up in stacks against the side of the spare attic room. Gwen spent ages just looking at their titles. There were a large number of adventure stories about cowboys, planes and spies. She'd try one or two, she thought. Further back in the room, there were also other kinds. Books on things she'd never thought they could write books about, like carp fishing, archaeology and photography. At the top of the pile was a thick volume called

Traditions, Superstitions, and Folklore. She was taking it down to see if it had any pictures, when she heard a shout from downstairs. Eddie was at the kitchen door.

It was already midday. Once again time had disappeared.

She clattered down the stairs, aware that she'd said nothing of Eddie's plan to Aunt Tiny. He was leaning against the doorframe just out of the way of the drips coming off the overloaded guttering. But outside it was bright. The rain had stopped and the sun was even stronger, reflecting off the puddles in the yard.

"Are you ready?" Eddie looked her up and down.

"No, sorry. Give me a minute."

She didn't even know where her aunt was to ask if she could take some food. She turned awkwardly on the stairs and called.

"Auntie?"

"I think she's outside. Do you want me to tell her we are leaving?" Eddie asked.

Gwen nodded and hopped off the bottom step. She scoured the kitchen. There was the loaf of bread. If she buttered a couple of slices she could take a jam sandwich. It would do. She started cutting the loaf.

Eddie came back.

"She says you have to be back by tea time, and you can cut a piece of cheese from the larder."

They set off eventually, having forced Gwen's food into Eddie's school satchel. Most of the space was taken up by a large and heavy glass bottle.

"That's important," Eddie said. "It's not just for drinking."

"What's it for?"

But Eddie wasn't ready to give up his secrets yet. He scratched a scab on his elbow and hoisted the satchel onto his back.

"You'll see," he said, leading the way up the drive towards the hill. Sensing there was a chance of a walk, Boo appeared from the back of the stable and followed the procession, but Gwen was pleased to see that he stuck to her side rather than Eddie's.

They climbed up the steep hill hardly saying a word. On either side of the road the hedges dripped and shone. It was not easy keeping up with Eddie's long legs, but Gwen was determined not to fall behind. By the time they reached the farm lane with its sign and milk cans, she was hot and red in the face. Thirty yards beyond it, Eddie stopped as they entered the shade of the trees.

"Down this path now," he said, and led them into the wood running along the ridge that she'd noticed on her very first day in Shropshire. Gwen almost immediately tripped over a root, but righted herself in time. It would be so humiliating to fall on the threshold of the wood.

Eddie was already quite far ahead, and she didn't want him to think she was slow. She picked her way over the debris on the path as quickly as she could. A cool breeze moved the leaves around her, and Gwen began to feel better.

There was another feeling too, one that she couldn't quite pinpoint. It was as if she'd entered a library, or an old church, where she must be very quiet. She tried not to crack sticks underfoot as she went. Eddie did not turn around at all. The strap of his satchel squeaked every time he moved in a certain direction, but otherwise the only sounds were birds, the breeze moving the leaves above them and the occasional drip of rain from the canopy.

As they walked down the ridge through the trees, the view across the wide valley below opened up. The large hill was not fully visible, but in the middle distance she was sure she could see the edge of her aunt's house. And beyond, wasn't that Eddie's farm?

There was also a group of farm buildings further down the road that she hadn't noticed before.

The trees around her looked wild and neglected, not like the plantations near Cannock she had visited with school. Many were covered in twisting ivy, with stumps that had grown countless stems. The ground was a chaotic collection of branches and green leaves. It smelt rich and fresh, like just-turned earth and cut flower stems.

Considering how many questions he had asked her yesterday, Eddie was being very quiet. As they went further down the narrow path, Gwen could see clear sky through the trees to her right. So that must be the top of the ridge. But what was beyond it? A fallen log nearly tripped her up, and she jerked her attention back to the path.

It was changing direction, turning to the right at a large tree. Gwen slowed to a halt in front of it. It was large, old and gnarled, and it reminded her of the oak tree with the strange wooden creature in the painting. There was a deep black hole between its lumpy roots. She bent down to look inside, feeling almost giddy, as if she were being pulled off balance.

"Come on Gwen, we're nearly there!" Eddie called from down the path. "It's not much further."

She stood up quickly and backed away from the tree. Eddie was waiting for her, beckoning. Above her, a cawing flock of black birds soared overhead, dropping down towards the field below, heading for Netherwood.

Gwen realized her hands had tightened into fists. She tried to relax them, but the backs were pricking unpleasantly. She scratched at the pink scar across her palm, but it didn't help. Eddie was walking again, his arms swinging, looking unperturbed.

Gwen looked around for Boo. There was no sight, nor sound of him.

"Eddie, where's Boo?"

"Huh?" He looked back. "I thought he was with you."

"He was a minute ago." The pricking started down her spine.

"Boo!" she shouted. "Boozle!" She'd never heard Aunt Tiny call him, so had no idea what he answered to, but the man who lived two doors down from them in Erdington had a Jack Russell, so she tried:

"Here boy!"

Nothing.

Eddie whistled a long note followed by two short blasts. A raucous flapping came from the wood on the ridge, and a large, brightly coloured bird shot out of the undergrowth like anti-aircraft fire.

"That will be him," Eddie said, confidently. "No dog can resist a hiding pheasant."

Boo came clattering down towards them. He was panting hard.

"Was that a pheasant?" Gwen had never seen a live one. "It was beautiful."

"A cock pheasant. They used to be common as rats here," Eddie said, "but no shooting since the war started. That one must be quite old."

Boo was nosing in her hand, looking for food or something. She scratched behind his ears.

"Do you think it's safe to take him through here?"

Eddie laughed.

"Worse that could happen is he runs after a pheasant and goes over the edge of the cliff into the quarry." Eddie pointed towards the ridge. "But he'd have to be a stupid dog to do that, and you told me he was clever." He smirked at Gwen.

Gwen ignored this comment.

"There's a quarry over there? What do they dig out?"

"Limestone. Here, I'll show you. We're nearly at the best place."

He left the path and headed up towards the top of the ridge. Gwen followed, looking for each footfall. The ground was very uneven and covered with fallen branches. They came round an outcrop of rock and saplings into a carved-out gully with a tall holly tree at its head. Eddie turned around and spread his arms.

"Your very own fossil quarry." He went over to the exposed rock. "Here, look."

At first Gwen couldn't see what he was pointing at in the rough grey rock. She peered at it, nervous that she would miss what Eddie found so obvious. It was full of small shapes, shells, fronds, stems, whorls of segmented armour – all the same grey-white colour. The rock was made of these plants and creatures, preserved as if frozen in a block of ice.

"Sometimes you can find a rock with a larger ammonite, but most have these small fossils. Can you see the stem?" She nodded as he pointed out a cross-section that looked like a pipe. "These are four hundred and fifty million years old."

"How can you tell?"

He laughed.

"I can't. I found out about it from a geology book. They are even older than those dinosaurs you saw.

Look." He took a small hammer out of the pocket of his short trousers and began tapping around another section of the stone that was sticking out slightly. "It takes a while, but if you get it out, you will be the first person to see these animals in millions of years. Don't stand too close though; the bits of rock can fly into your eyes."

She watched him as he worked on it, his face intent. After a few moments, the section came out like a brick from a wall.

"There!" Eddie said happily. "Get the bottle of water, and let's see what we've got."

Gwen rummaged in the satchel and pulled it out. Boo was nosing around the undergrowth below them, finding rabbit holes.

She handed the bottle to Eddie, but he gave it back to her.

"You do the pouring. Your clothes will get splashed otherwise. Just a little at a time. I've got a toothbrush here to scrub it." He'd replaced the hammer in his hand with a small brush. He put the section of stone on the ground and squatted on his heels, brush poised.

As she poured the water, the stone darkened and the shapes stood out more clearly.

"Stop." Eddie scrubbed at the stone with his little brush for a moment. "More water now."

She poured again.

"That's enough."

He held the stone up for her to see. It was crawling with shapes.

"What's that?" she asked, pointing to a branching tree-like thing with lots of holes like a pincushion.

"A piece of coral. One of my favourites. Look at this one; it's part of a sponge like you'd use in the bath," he laughed, shaking his hair out of his eyes.

"Is that a snail?"

"Yes, a sea snail. All these plants and animals lived in a tropical sea, because all this land used to be south of the equator."

"That can't be true," Gwen said. "That's thousands of miles away!"

"It is true. This is some of the oldest rock in the world, and it used to be much further south." Eddie was still looking at the fossils. He pointed to one that was a round tube. "This one was a bit like an anemone."

He handed the stone to Gwen. She sat down on the ground and stared at it. There were so many. Little scallop shells and sections of plants that looked a bit like bamboo. Eddie was bent over the satchel, undoing the buckles. Gwen looked up at the rock face.

"Is it all like this?"

"It is here. It changes down in the valley. Even around your stream in Netherwood there are different fossils." He held up the wrapped sandwiches. "Are you hungry?"

"Mmmm." Gwen looked around for Boo. He wasn't there. "Boo's gone again. Can you whistle him?"

Eddie stood up and blew a long blast and three short ones.

"If Boo's that clever, he should know Morse Code."

"Oh ha, ha," Gwen said, getting up herself.

Again, she had that strange pricking feeling on her hands and neck. It would be awful to lose her aunt's dog, especially as she believed that Anders had sent him.

That was not something Gwen could explain to Eddie, however.

Eddie saw her expression and whistled again.

Faintly, in the distance, there was a high-pitched whine. Then a short bark, again high-pitched.

"He's stuck somewhere. That's the sound they make when they are frightened," Eddie said, already running down onto the path, the satchel and sandwiches abandoned.

Gwen raced after him. The sound had come from further north and up the hill. Perhaps the path would turn that way.

"Boo," she shouted, hoping he would keep barking so they could locate him. "Boo!"

There was another short bark and a whine, like brakes screeching.

Eddie pointed into the trees, barely slowing down.

"Up there, by the bluebell clearing."

They stumbled up the hill, scrambling over fallen trees and stones, and burst through the shade into a small patch of sunlight at the top, a glade surrounded by elder trees laden with berries.

The barking was loud and frantic, but at first Gwen couldn't see where Boo was. She shouted for him again, but her voice seemed to die as it left her mouth.

She looked at Eddie who had stopped on the edge of the clearing. His mouth was open, panting a little, his eyes wide.

Gwen clapped her hands and cleared her throat to call the dog. The feeling of pricking was making the hair stand up on her head.

"Where is he?" she whispered

Eddie took a step forward and whistled.

This time they heard growling. It came from the other side of the clearing where a large yew tree threw a patch of darkness on the ground.

They sprinted across the clearing towards it.

He was there, standing with his paws on the yew trunk, growling and scratching at it, saliva dripping from his muzzle, his eyes wild.

"Boozle!" Gwen called, but it came out as a croak. Her chest ached from running. She approached him, holding out her hand, but Boo didn't look at her. It was as if he were caught around his legs by an invisible rope.

"He must be after something in the tree," Eddie said, his voice high and strange. He was standing stock-still, staring at the twitching, growling dog.

Gwen went slowly towards Boo. As she came under the yew, it became cold – winter cold. She looked up into the heavy branches. At first she could see nothing but dark green needles and red berries.

An even colder draught made her shiver violently, but Gwen crossed her arms and stared up again. A long pale arm, fingers rigid and outstretched, was reaching down from the middle of the yew towards the dog.

Gwen's heart pounded in her chest. The white fingers were pointing straight at Boo. He had stopped barking and was staring upwards, mouth open as if in a trance.

"Boo, come away," she whispered between chattering teeth, reaching out for the collar around his neck.

As soon as her fingers touched his fur, he turned his head and whimpered. He seemed to go slack for a moment, as if the string holding him up had been cut, then he turned from the tree and ran, tail between his legs, down the hill.

Gwen didn't dare look up into the tree again.

"Go after him!" she shouted at Eddie, and, at his heels, she ran across the bright clearing after the dog.

Chapter 6

They managed to keep the dog in sight for a few moments, but when he reached the path he was too fast. Boo was racing back the way they had come, as if chased by a tiger.

"He's going home," Eddie panted, stopping after a while. Gwen bent over; her lungs felt about to burst. She straightened up and coughed. "Are you all right?" Eddie asked.

"Yes." Gwen wiped her forehead with a shaking hand. "What was that," she gasped, "that thing that had Boo stuck to the tree?"

Eddie shook his head.

"I don't know. Dogs get all excited about squirrels and things. He probably gave one a good chase and didn't want to let it go."

Eddie hadn't seen the thing. He was walking back towards the gully and their sandwiches as if everything was fine.

"But why did he sound so scared?" Gwen asked his back. "He was frantic."

"Do you have a dog at home?" Eddie said, sounding impatient.

"No."

"Well, I have three. Dogs just do strange things. They can hear a lot of noises that we can't hear at all. Maybe the branches of the tree were rubbing together. Maybe there was a whole nest of baby squirrels. Maybe he was bitten by a badger. Who knows?"

"It wasn't any of those things. There was something in that tree that was holding him. And it felt very cold."

Eddie turned to look at her.

"Don't be silly," he said. But he looked alarmed.

Gwen bit her lip.

"I want to go home now."

Eddie shrugged and led them silently back to the gully where the fossil rock lay, still wet, on the ground. He pulled the sandwiches out of the satchel, opened the packet and held it out to her.

"Listen, you live in the city. You're not used to animals and woods," he said, taking one when she shook her head. "I've been in here at dusk when the owls are screeching, but nothing bad happened." He gestured at the undergrowth with his one free hand.

Now that they were back by his school satchel and not by the dark yew tree, he was regaining some of his swagger.

Gwen said nothing. She was too close to tears, and she wasn't going to cry here in the wood in front of an older boy.

"Have a drink of water. That was quite a run," he said with his mouth full, pointing to the bottle that was propped next to a log.

Gwen went over to it and poured some in her mouth. It dripped down her chin and onto her top. She handed it to him and took a deep breath.

"You can have my sandwiches. I want to check that Boo has gone home." She turned to walk out of the gully.

"Wait a minute, I'll come with you. Just let me pack this up."

She stopped but didn't turn round.

"He'll be fine, you know," Eddie said as he shouldered the satchel. Gwen set off down the track.

"He will be lying in your kitchen or by the stable, I bet."

Gwen kept walking.

The sun was dipping west. In the valley, a tractor was working its way across a golden field. If she strained her ears, Gwen could just hear the sound of its chugging engine. It reminded her of the train that her mother had travelled home in. Going back to the crowds and streets and terraces of houses, where the bombers went at night.

She walked faster, blinking hard. Why when she looked forward to something was it always ruined? Why were there always so many worries?

"Are you sure you don't want the last sandwich?" Eddie held it over her shoulder.

"No thank you."

She could hear him chewing it quickly as he walked. They were almost at the road. When they reached it, they had to stop to let a large car go past. Its exhaust fumes nearly set Gwen coughing again.

"Look at that. A new Vauxhall Twelve. Who could that be?" Eddie said, watching as it disappeared around the bend. He sounded as if he should know everyone driving on this road. "Which school are you going to, by the way?"

Gwen was taken aback.

"I don't know. Are there many to choose from?" It seemed odd that a place with so few people might need more than one school.

"Not many, but a few. Used to be one just over the fields from you, but that closed years ago. There's one in Sheinton and one in Much Wenlock, for a start. That's the bigger one."

"I was hoping to go home before school starts."

Eddie raised his eyebrows at her.

"All the evacuees that came in the early summer are expected to stay until next year. The ones in Wenlock come from Liverpool, and they sound even sillier than you," he said slyly.

"You're the one 'as sounds silly," she countered, trying to imitate his accent. "What's that big hill over there?"

"Called the Wrekin. It's pretty famous. Been in some poems."

"I don't really like poetry. Last year, our teacher made us memorize some." It had been a poet called Keats who used lots of big words. Mr Grosset had caned those who made more than three mistakes, which Gwen had.

"Why is it famous?"

"A British tribe used to live on top. They fought the invading Romans and lost."

They had reached the turning to Netherwood.

Gwen peered down at the house. She guessed it was around three o'clock, and Aunt Tiny would be undisturbable in her studio. They opened the gate and walked down towards the yard.

"There he is. The rascal," Eddie said.

Boo was stretched out in the shade thrown by the stable, fast asleep already. Gwen went over to him. He seemed very still. She stroked his chest and fondled his soft ear. His tail wagged. He lifted his head a little and sniffed her, then lay back down.

"He's exhausted," she said.

"Got too hot racing around like a puppy. Do you know how old he is?"

Gwen shook her head.

"He could be old, judging by those teeth." Boo had his mouth open as he slept, exposing worn and blackened stumps. "Anyway, my dad will want my help with the milking. Here, I thought you might like to keep this." Eddie opened the satchel and took out the piece of rock he had extracted from the hill. It was cool in her hot hands. "Don't be imagining any more scary things now," he said, walking across the yard and out of view.

That evening Gwen stayed up later, and Aunt Tiny read out a letter that had arrived from her mother. Gwen guessed that there were things in the letter Aunt Tiny did not want her to know, otherwise she would have let her read it herself.

Along with the admonitions to be good and keep her things tidy, her mother mentioned that she'd had a letter from Daddy and that he was beginning to feel better, and that no bombs had dropped near them since Gwen had left. The west of Birmingham had been targeted instead. Her mother was working even longer hours in the technical drawing office of the Birmingham Small Arms factory to meet the huge demand for rifles.

Aunt Tiny read out the last paragraph:

"'Gwen, you must stay there where it is safe and begin the school year. When all the German planes are destroyed, you can come home, and we will all be together again. I will come to visit you one weekend, as soon as I can.' And she has signed it with love and a few kisses."

Gwen pushed her tin mug around on the bare polished boards of the kitchen table.

"What school will I go to?" she asked.

"I thought the one in Much Wenlock would be best," Aunt Tiny said. "And your mother agreed. It has four classes so should be better than the little village one where all the ages are in together. It will be more like what you are used to, and you can walk up the lane with Eddie."

Gwen didn't say anything.

"Unless you don't like Eddie? I thought you were getting on well as you went on that picnic together."

"It wasn't a picnic. He just wanted to show me the fossils in the woods up there." Gwen said, gesturing behind her to where the wood was no doubt growing dark, and the owls were waking up.

"Didn't you enjoy it?" Aunt Tiny asked, looking at Gwen with her head on one side.

"Boo came with us, but he went off and got scared in the woods, then he ran home. So we weren't there very long."

Aunt Tiny took a breath and held it for a moment, letting it out slowly. She smiled rather strangely.

"Mmmm. That sounds like Boo. He is an excitable boy. Do you know what scared him?"

Gwen looked down at the table.

"It was something in a tree. Eddie thought it was a squirrel."

Aunt Tiny paused and folded her hands.

"Oh, well. That's not too frightening, but perhaps it's best not to take Boo when you go to those woods," she said, leaning forward. "He doesn't always do as he's told, and I wouldn't want him getting you into trouble with the owner."

"Who's that?"

"A very grumpy man by the name of Mr Morrison. Lives down in Ironbridge, but he sits in his hut in the middle of that quarry, and if he sees people coming out of the wood he shouts to high heaven!" Aunt Tiny raised her hands in the air above her head. "He claims he doesn't want people there because of the danger of the quarry, but everyone thinks it's just because he is a miserly old misery-guts who doesn't like people on his land. Stay away from the top of the ridge and away from the quarry when you go with Eddie, and you'll be fine."

Her aunt got up from her chair and stretched her long back and arms.

"Now I feel like playing a bit of piano before bed. Would you like to come to the parlour?"

For nearly an hour, her aunt played through several old music hall songs and encouraged Gwen to learn the words. 'Daddy Wouldn't Buy Me a Bow Wow' was her favourite:

I love my little cat I do
With soft black silky hair.
It comes with me each day to school
And sits upon the chair.
When teacher says 'Why do you bring
That little pet of yours?'
I tell her that I bring my cat
Along with me because
Daddy wouldn't buy me a bow-wow, bow-wow!
Daddy wouldn't buy me a bow-wow, bow-wow!
I've got a little cat and I'm very fond of that,
But I'd rather have a bow-wow, wow, wow, wow.

"I didn't know you had such a good voice, Gwen." Aunt Tiny said, turning to her when they finished. "They'll be wanting you in the church choir if the organist finds out."

Gwen hid her smile behind her hand and followed her aunt into the kitchen. They lit their candles and put the blinds on the windows. Boo was under the table.

"Can Boo sleep in my room?" Gwen asked, snapping her fingers to encourage him up.

"He can if he wants to," her aunt said. "But he is a restless sleeper, always racing around in his dreams, so don't be surprised if he wakes you up. And he might want to come down to me later, so leave the door ajar."

Aunt Tiny led the way up the stairs and said goodnight at her bedroom door. Then Gwen and Boo went up the next flight of stairs together.

Chapter 7

The night was long and confusing. Gwen thought she heard planes overhead, but when she tried to get up to look out of the window, her body wouldn't obey. She was dreaming.

Next she was back in the wood near the elder glade. The sun was low on the horizon, and something was running through the trees over her head. Something tall and lithe that was about to turn and look at her. And if it looked at her, Gwen knew it would take her. She ran down the steep bank and crouched under the large oak, hiding her face. All she could hear was mirthless, high-pitched laughter. She woke up with cold sweat on her forehead.

Boo had started the night on the rug by her bed, but at some point he had climbed up and was a heavy weight across one of her feet. She wriggled out from under him, but her foot had gone to sleep and she had to hop around the dark room while the pins and needles came and went. There was light coming from the gap in the bedroom door, so it must be morning.

Gwen went to the window and took down the blind. It was very early; the light was still pale and weak. In the pen, the hens were just emerging from the henhouse. The forest was a large dark mass below her. She shivered in her thin cotton nightgown and ran back to the bed. The dog had gone, leaving lots of white and brown hairs on the bedspread. Gwen climbed back under the covers and pulled them over her head. She felt strange, as if her head was stretched out and she was looking at herself from a distance.

If only she could stop the dreams, she wouldn't feel so odd and tired. She pushed the covers down and sighed. There was no chance of getting back to sleep. If she'd been at home, she would have read a fairy story, a favourite that she'd read a hundred times before. They always helped when she was upset. But her mother had said that books were too heavy to pack, and so they had stayed behind in her small bedroom, where they were more than likely to be bombed and burnt to a crisp.

Gwen looked at the door, remembering the room full of books she'd started exploring the day before. Hadn't there been a book of fairy stories or something like that?

She crept across the hall to the other door, opened it and stepped in. The room was quite dark, but she could just make out the stacks of books and one thick volume on the floor by the door where she had abandoned it when Eddie arrived.

It was heavy, with a dark leather cover embossed with gold lettering. Gwen took it into the better light of the hallway.

"Traditions, Superstitions, and Folklore," she murmured, feeling disappointed. It was just a list of things that people used to believe. Maybe there were other books that would have proper stories in them, but it would have to do. She didn't want to wake Aunt Tiny by thumping around upstairs.

Back by her window, she opened the book at random, close to the beginning, and began to read about birds.

Birds are soul bringers. Sacred birds include the woodpecker, owl, cuckoo, stork and swallow. And there was a curious rhyme: *Robin redbreast and Jenny wren are God Almighty's cock and hen.*

Her mother wouldn't like that. She had a horror of birds, and, whenever a pigeon came near her in the street, she would cover her head and run away.

Gwen turned a few pages to a section about trees.

Apparently mistletoe was *botanic lightning*, which protected the homestead from fire and other disasters because it grew on oak, a sacred and magical tree. Oaks were everywhere around here, but she hadn't spotted any mistletoe. With all the leaves still on the trees, you'd have to climb or fly to find it. A bit further down the page there was a small sketch of a twig with leaves and berries.

The ash and the rowan have power over witches, fairies and imps of darkness.

The rowan had red berries. So did the yew, but whatever was in that yew tree yesterday had not felt friendly. Perhaps the tree itself was the problem. Yews were often seen in graveyards, which didn't bode well. She cast her eye over the next few pages. Nothing about yew trees, but divining rods, whatever they were, must be made of hazel or rowan. And another piece of useful information – fern seed could make a person invisible.

She shut the book impatiently. Downstairs the ping of bedsprings indicated that Aunt Tiny was getting up, and the sound of scampering down the stairs was Boo running ahead of her to wait for his breakfast.

Gwen's tummy rumbled. She would run out and do the chickens quickly. Perhaps she'd be able to have an egg on toast for breakfast.

Aunt Tiny was boiling the kettle when she came back inside.

"You are up early and with five eggs already. That is eggcellent," she quipped.

"Mum says that one too." Gwen put the eggs in the basket and went to the sink to wash her hands.

"It was one of our father's favourite puns," Aunt Tiny said, putting the teapot on the table. "Now, after a good breakfast, I thought we'd go to town to do the shopping you will need for school. I'll be busy next week with a commission, so best to get it done and then it's not a worry at the last minute." She went to the egg basket. "Would you like scrambled or fried?"

"Scrambled please," Gwen said, although she preferred boiled. Different feelings were taking turns in her mind, like a carousel. Excitement to see the town and buy new things, and fright at the thought of having to go to a strange school with no one she knew.

In the end it was hard to finish her egg and toast because her stomach was full of butterflies. Aunt Tiny had gone to get ready, so she didn't see Gwen give the rest of her breakfast to the dog.

She'd told Gwen a man was going to give them a lift in his car, but that they must walk to his house in Much Wenlock. Boo was not allowed to come. He watched them through the window as they set off up the drive, barking dejectedly.

"Thank goodness it's not raining like yesterday," Aunt Tiny remarked, closing the gate behind them.

It felt much longer ago than that, Gwen thought. Since seeing the strange creature in the yew tree, she felt older, as if months had passed. But it was a beautiful morning and not too hot. The smell of mown grass filled the air. As they started up the hill, Gwen realized that they were going to walk past the Quarry Wood on their way to Much Wenlock, and a tremor went through her.

"I've packed your gas mask in here with mine, Gwen," Aunt Tiny said, patting her large shopping bag. "There are lots of defence volunteers in Shrewsbury who will fine you if you don't carry them. Mainly old men who are very pleased with their new authority."

Gwen had completely forgotten her mask for the past few days. It was associated with the smoke and fear of the city, the rushing to the air raid shelters and the drills at school which made them all giggle with nerves, not with the forests and fields of the countryside.

They had passed the farm and were approaching the path that led into the wood. The birdsong coming from the trees seemed very loud to Gwen, the notes almost like words she could understand. The sound echoing in her mind was making her dizzy. She shook her head and looked up at Aunt Tiny. Their eyes met. Her aunt's were quizzical and concerned. Gwen looked away quickly.

"How long will it take to get to town in the car?" she asked.

"Probably only forty minutes or so. It depends how many stops Mr Williams has to make on the way. He's a salesman of brushes, and rather eccentric with it, but very nice too."

That ended up being a good summary of Mr Williams, a dapper, elderly man with a Morris Minor full of boxes and assorted equipment. He sang hymns in a quavering tenor almost continuously throughout the journey.

Gwen could see very little of the countryside as she had a large box full of carpet brushes on her lap. Aunt Tiny was sitting in the front and telling Mr Williams about Gwen's voice.

"You will want her in the choir when you hear her, I promise, Mr Williams. She is a proper nightingale."

"Ah, will I now?" he said, rather loftily. "We will have to see about that on Sunday."

And so Gwen gathered that Mr Williams was the choirmaster as well as a brush salesman.

After showing their Identity cards to the wardens on the bridge, they were allowed to drive into the town, where Mr Williams was making several deliveries. He stopped in front of a general hardware shop. Aunt Tiny agreed to meet him there in two hours and marched Gwen up a steep hill lined with old timbered buildings.

The shops were small compared with Birmingham, but the proprietors were friendly, although some looked askance at her aunt who was wearing bright blue shoes, a scarlet red skirt and an emerald green hat.

Gwen's old pinafore was deemed to be acceptable for the Wenlock school, but she would require new socks and a white shirt. These could be found at a local haberdasher Aunt Tiny knew close to the river. Her aunt also needed some special tools that were not available in Much Wenlock, so they went to the ironmonger.

When all that was done and Aunt Tiny's bag was full, they walked back towards the bridge they had crossed. The streets were busier now, and Gwen felt tired and empty.

"Shall we have a quick cup of tea and a bun before we meet Mr Williams?" her aunt asked, looking at her watch. "We have more than half an hour." And soon they were installed at a table in a crowded tearoom close to the bridge. The door was wedged open and the sounds of buses and crowds filled the room.

"You are very quiet today, Gwen. Are you missing home?"

Gwen shook her head. She didn't want to talk about that.

Aunt Tiny took a bite out of her teacake and wiped the butter off her lips with a napkin.

"Is it the start of school that is worrying you?"

Gwen hesitated, then nodded.

Aunt Tiny stirred another lump of sugar into her tea and passed the bowl to Gwen.

"I'm sure Eddie will look after you. I know he is a boy, but he has a very good heart, and –"

"But he's going to be in a different class," Gwen blurted out, "and he thinks I'm silly."

Aunt Tiny smiled broadly.

"No, it's not a big enough school for that. You older children are all in together in these small towns. Right up to thirteen when some will go to the woodworking and domestic science classrooms. And as to whether he thinks you are silly," Aunt Tiny tapped Gwen's hand with the tip of her finger, "that's just what boys are like. Even if they really like and admire you, they will call you 'silly' and make fun of you. In fact the more they like you, the more they will do that." She sighed. "It can be thoroughly annoying, but that's the way it is. Best thing to do is give as good as you get, then most of the boys will think of you as a good laugh and include you in their games."

Gwen tried to smile to reassure her aunt, but her worries remained. Whatever was in the Quarry wood wasn't playing a game that included Eddie – just her.

She picked up her cup, spilling tea on the saucer with her unsteady hand.

"I'm afraid you'll have to drink up," Aunt Tiny said. "We are out of time."

The journey home was more comfortable. Most of the boxes had been delivered, so Gwen had a view out of the window. The Wrekin hill stayed in sight almost all the way back to Mr Williams' house in Much Wenlock.

Chapter 8

Over the next few days, Gwen found a sort of rhythm to life at her aunt's house. In the morning she would read and do her jobs; in the afternoon Eddie would meet her at the stream. He did not suggest another trip to the Quarry Wood, and Gwen did not mention it. It seemed that if she went again, she would have to go on her own. They never spoke about what happened that day either, as if by mutual agreement.

After supper she and her aunt would sing and play old music hall songs until bedtime. Despite the pleasant days, Gwen's dreams were still frightening.

Although she would have preferred one of her own familiar books, she found herself reading her way compulsively through several chapters of *Traditions, Superstitions, and Folklore*, as if she were looking for something in particular. Then, in her dreams, the spirits and creatures of the book would come to full and frightening life in Quarry Wood. When Gwen woke confused and exhausted, the only comfort was the warm and furry Boo lying next to her. Or, sometimes, on top of her.

On Sunday her aunt made a special breakfast. Gwen enjoyed the bacon but eyed the mushrooms suspiciously. The book had lots to say about mushrooms and toadstools, especially about how they could cause a painful death. Her aunt was eating them enthusiastically and seemed fine, however, so Gwen finished her plateful, taking care not to get any grease on her Sunday dress.

"Mr Williams wants you there early so he can hear your voice and decide where to put you in the choir," Aunt Tiny said. She herself was dressed rather peculiarly in her scarlet red skirt and sturdy work boots.

"Are you coming to church too, Auntie?"

"I will drop you off, then I'm going to have a cup of tea with an old friend who needs some company. Church and I had a falling-out several years ago, so it's probably best if I don't stay for the service." Aunt Tiny pressed her lips together and raised her eyebrows. "As long as I make sure that you go, your mother should be happy enough. And after today, you will be able to walk yourself up there."

Gwen felt a bit sick. She would have to attend a new church on her own, surrounded by hundreds of people she didn't know. She was bound to do something wrong.

"Now don't look so down in the mouth," Aunt Tiny said firmly. "Not everyone in the world goes to church, despite what you may have been told by dear old Mrs Judd." She got up from the table and took her plate to the sink. "Mr Williams will look after you. He has the choir well disciplined, so a nice girl like you won't have any trouble at all."

Gwen was not sure she liked the sound of that.

As it turned out, they arrived before Mr Williams at the parish room and had to wait at the door. Her aunt smiled as people walked past and nodded 'Good Morning'. Whatever the falling-out with the church had been, her aunt seemed determined not to show any sign of it.

Mr Williams eventually appeared, swinging a walking stick and humming. When he saw Gwen, his well-groomed moustache twitched upwards.

"Ah, the nightingale. I've been looking forward to this. I hope you won't disappoint." He unlocked the door and ushered her in.

The room was small and stuffy, full of old wooden chairs, a piano, a small kitchen sink, an electric ring and cupboard. On the wall was a framed, decorated Bible verse: *Sing unto the Lord a new song.*

"Now, stand by the piano, and we will do some scales. The choir will be here at any moment."

Mr Williams quickly established that she was a soprano and gave her an arrangement of 'All creatures that on earth do dwell' to sing. It made her think of the chickens for some reason, and she had to be very strict with herself or she would have started laughing.

When she'd finished, he stood up, put his hands on the top of the upright piano and looked at her sternly.

"God has given you a lovely voice, so now it is your responsibility to use it. I expect you at choir practice after school every Thursday without fail, and on Sundays you are to arrive half an hour before the eleven o'clock service. Mrs Lloyd will find you a robe."

The door opened suddenly. Two boys and a girl stood on the threshold. They were slightly out of breath and stared hard at her as they sat down. More children of various ages followed, until fifteen chairs were full.

"Here they all are, except for the usual latecomer," Mr Williams said cheerfully. "This is Gwen; she is from Birmingham and will sing in the soprano section. Make her welcome." The children whispered to each other, and someone giggled. "Go and sit down over there," Mr Williams said, waving towards the group of girls. Gwen had just found a chair when the door banged open again, and a young boy ran in to universal tutting.

"Rhys, you are not *as* late as usual," Mr Williams announced. "That is a sign of improvement. Sit near Gwen. She is also a soprano."

The boy was small, wiry, and had black hair slicked down across his forehead like a miniature man. When he smiled, his grin was full of gaps. He sat down in the chair behind her.

As the rehearsal started, Rhys began pulling on her plaits in time to 'All things bright and beautiful' while Mr Williams was absorbed with the alto section. The girl sitting next to him reached over and slapped his hand. She was a bit shorter than Gwen, but she looked older, her expression self-assured.

"Leave her alone, you little pest," she said in a loud whisper as they all stood up to put on their choir robes. "Or I'll tell your Ma."

Rhys checked that no one was looking and stuck out his tongue at the girl before going to the rail and taking down the shortest robe.

"He's an awful pain but should settle down," the girl said to Gwen, pulling a blue robe over her head. "He always tries it on with new people. His mother is a washerwoman and has a very strong arm. Rhys knows about it if she gives him a slap. He has got a voice like an angel though, which is completely unfair considering what a little devil he is."

"Thanks." Gwen tried to smile. "What's your name?"

"Rosie. I don't know where Mrs Lloyd is, but here, this is the robe that Sarah used to wear before she died of TB." She gave Gwen a sly look out of the corner of her eye. "It should fit you."

She took it off the hanger and handed it to Gwen, watching with an amused expression while she struggled to get the robe over her head. But it did fit her quite well.

"Here, you have to tie the cord this special way around your waist."

"Quiet everyone. It's time to go in," Mr Williams called. He opened the door and the sound of church bells became loud and thrilling. "Rosie, partner the new girl and make her aware of the rules. But *sotto voce*," he said, with a crooked index finger to his lips.

The line of children moved out of the door two by two.

Rosie gave Gwen an appraising look.

"You been in a choir before?"

Gwen nodded.

"I bet ours is better," she said, and went ahead into the bright sunshine.

It wasn't better, but it wasn't bad, and when they were back in the choir room getting out of their robes, Gwen thought it wise to tell Rosie that she was impressed. Rosie just nodded.

"Your voice is quite good," she admitted grudgingly. "I think you should try to be a bit louder next time, once you've got used to the music."

"Where do you live?" Gwen asked.

"Just round the corner; my father is the schoolmaster. How old are you?"

Gwen felt her stomach jump. If the daughter was this bossy, what was the schoolmaster like?

"Ten."

"I'm nearly ten," Rosie said. "We'll be in the same class. My father will like you. He hates noisy children. Bye."

And she was out of the door and gone.

"How was the choir? I assume Mr Williams was happy to have you?" Aunt Tiny asked when she arrived at the door a few moments later.

"Fine," Gwen said.

"Just fine?"

Aunt Tiny was carrying a large basket in her left hand. It seemed to be heavy, as she was walking bent over sideways.

"I met a girl called Rosie," Gwen said. "What's in the basket?"

"Ah, Rosie Brown? The schoolmaster's daughter?"

Gwen nodded.

"I see." Aunt Tiny chuckled. "She is a character. Her father is fair, I'm told. Nothing to worry about, although I do understand your ambivalence."

"What does that mean?"

"Ambivalence means when you are not sure how to think about something, if you don't know if it's good or bad."

That was the case with most things at the moment, except Hitler. He was definitely evil. But the rest of life seemed to be a confusing mixture.

"You don't have to go to choir, you know. Your mother didn't say anything about that."

But to just sit in church on her own would be even worse than being with Rhys and the self-assured Rosie Brown.

"No, it's fine. I want to go," Gwen said. Something in the basket was moving, and her aunt swapped it over to her other hand.

"See if you can guess what's in the basket. When we get home, you can see if you're right."

"Is it alive?" Gwen asked.

"Oh, are we playing Twenty Questions? Very well. Yes."

Gwen looked at her aunt's boots. There was a thick caking of mud on the heels.

"Does it have wings?"

"No," her aunt laughed. "It would look so funny with wings."

So it wasn't a duck.

"Does it have four legs?"

"Yes."

"Is it woolly?"

"No. Although it does like wool."

"Oh, you gave it away!" Gwen cried.

"You are just too quick," Aunt Tiny retorted.

"It's a cat!"

"Yes, but not just any cat. The cat in this basket is a queen of cats, by the name of Cleopatra."

"Who is that?"

Gwen looked down at the basket curiously, but there were no chinks in the lid that showed what colour the cat was.

"An Egyptian Queen who was known for her regal beauty. She seduced a few Roman Generals. This Cleopatra is not quite so formidable. Although she will probably give Boozle a few scratches to remember."

"Why are you taking her home?"

"An old friend of mine is very ill. She's going into hospital for an operation, and when she comes out she doesn't think she will be able to look after the cat any more, so she offered her to me. I owe Mrs Almond a great deal, so I said 'of course' and after chasing the blessed cat around the garden pond for an hour, I finally caught her!"

A loud meow came from the basket, both mournful and angry. Aunt Tiny showed Gwen the inside of her arm. There was a long red scratch, still bleeding slightly.

"I think we will keep her in the house for a few days to stop her from trying to go home again," she said. "Apparently she likes people, or, at least, most of them."

"Do you think Boo will like her?"

"I'm not sure." Her aunt smiled crookedly. "Let's say he may well feel ambivalent towards her for a while."

When they got home, they let Boo outside and shut the door behind him.

"Gwen, go and check that no windows are open. Cats think nothing of jumping out of quite high windows," Aunt Tiny said, putting the basket on the kitchen floor.

When Gwen got back, out of breath from running all over the house, Aunt Tiny was putting a saucer of milk on the floor next to the basket, and Boo was scratching at the kitchen door, desperate to get in.

"Are you ready?"

Gwen nodded. Her aunt pulled the stick out of the loops and lifted the basket lid. A large tabby jumped out of the basket, stared around balefully and ran straight up the stairs. She was very fat, with bright green eyes.

They both looked up the staircase, listening. Cleopatra seemed to be scampering from room to room, looking for a way out.

"Well, here we are. The rule of three at work, I think. I have acquired a dog, a niece and a cat, all without asking. That must be the charm." Aunt Tiny winked at Gwen. "I reckon we should leave Cleo alone to explore for a while. Perhaps the smell of dinner cooking will bring her into the kitchen. As you can see, she likes her food."

"Can I go out to Boo?"

"Yes, good idea. Take him down to the stream and come back in an hour. Dinner will be ready by then."

Boo sniffed her all over when she slid out the door.

"I'm not the cat, daft dog. I haven't even touched her yet," she said, fondling his ears. He put his dusty paw on her dress and barked. Gwen looked down in dismay. She couldn't go to the stream in her Sunday best.

"I forgot to change, Auntie" she called, as she raced up the stairs.

Her bedroom door was open and sitting on her pillow was the cat, looking at her accusingly.

"Hello puss-cat," Gwen said, taking a step towards her and holding out her hand. The cat hissed and narrowed her eyes.

She sat there glowering while Gwen changed out of her dress and put on her old socks and shoes. Then, as she straightened up to leave the room, Cleo jumped off the bed and ran in front of her out of the door, her belly swaying.

By the time Gwen got to the bottom of the stairs, the cat was licking the milk from the saucer while Aunt Tiny peeled potatoes in the sink.

"There we are. She's going to be no trouble," her aunt said.

Based on events so far, Gwen thought that was overstating things.

She and Boo had only been at the stream for a few moments when Eddie came over the bridge. He'd not been at church because his family was Methodist. They went to chapel instead.

"How was choir?" he asked. The long piece of grass sticking out of the side of his mouth bobbed up and down as he talked.

Gwen straightened up and climbed onto the bridge. She sat down with her legs dangling over the stream, and Eddie sat next to her.

"There was a boy called Rhys who kept pulling my hair, and then a girl called Rosie helped me, but she was a bit . . ."

"Bossy?" Eddie suggested.

Gwen giggled.

"She's younger than me but she seemed so confident."

"She just likes being the little know-it-all," Eddie said magnanimously. "And she probably can't help it because her father is the schoolmaster."

"What's he like?"

Eddie spat the piece of grass into the stream.

"Painful, but not as bad as the last one. Mr Herring was a proper devil. And he smelt vile, like a rotten fish!"

Gwen giggled.

"What happened to him?"

"He signed up. Probably scaring a whole company of privates to death by now. They will have to wear their gas masks whenever he breathes on them. Mr Brown is shortsighted so he can't go to war. His spectacles are as thick as a book."

"We have a cat," Gwen said, not wanting to think about school any more. "My aunt was asked to look after her. She's as fat as a pig."

"What's her name?"

"Cleopatra. Apparently she was a queen who seduced Romans."

Eddie nodded knowingly.

"We might do her in history this year, if we're lucky. It's a good story. She killed herself with a snake. Let's hope your cat only kills mice."

He chuckled a little, plucked a frayed bit of wood from the plank he was sitting on and threw it into the stream.

Gwen was silent, staring down into the changing light on the water, the dark reflections of the trees overhead, and the strange, grasping branches that stretched and contracted in the rivulets.

"Eddie, when we went to rescue Boo from that yew tree, did you see anything strange?" She didn't look at him but felt him move uncomfortably beside her.

"What do you mean?"

"Didn't you see?" Gwen pleaded. "There was something in that tree that had Boo trapped, and when I touched him, it let go."

Eddie was silent. Then he whistled through his teeth, and Boo looked up from the hole he was digging in the undergrowth.

"It was strange the way the dog was behaving, but I didn't see anything. I should have gone over to him, not you, but something made it hard to move. Like my legs were rooted to the spot." He shivered.

Gwen lowered her eyes, in case her interest stopped him talking. Her breath was fast and shallow, remembering the cold power of the thing in the yew tree.

"That glade in the woods has always been a strange place," Eddie said. "In the spring it's full of bluebells, nothing else, no other flowers. There aren't many people who would walk through it at that time of year, even if they're not superstitious."

Gwen looked at Eddie's profile. He was not smiling.

"What happens if you walk through bluebells?"

"I don't know," he muttered, shaking his head. "Maybe the fairies take you. It's just stupid stories, isn't it?"

"But this wasn't a story. There was something real in that tree. You think so too, don't you?"

"Maybe." Eddie picked up a stick and began breaking bits off, throwing them one by one into the stream. Boo chased them all.

"Let's go back, without Boo," Gwen said, getting to her feet. "Let's go and see if anything's there."

"There won't be," Eddie insisted, not looking at her.

"But don't you think we should try to find out what it is? Like a scientist with the fossils. If you find something new, you investigate to find out what it is."

"Yes, but fossils are long dead and don't move around."

"You think it's gone?" Gwen asked, not voicing the other possibility; that the thing was still there, still dangerous.

"I don't know," he said crossly. "I just don't think it's a good idea to poke around in that tree." Eddie got up. "I've got to go back for my dinner. Mum will get cross if I'm late."

"I'm going to go up there anyway," Gwen said, as he stepped off the bridge. "You don't have to come. I know how to find it." She swallowed the lump in her throat. "I just want to know what it is, that's all."

Eddie didn't turn around. He threw the remains of the stick into the undergrowth.

"All right. I'll come with you. Not good for a young girl to go up there alone." And he stomped off towards the stile.

Gwen stayed on the bridge a while longer, fear and triumph coming and going. It hadn't been just her imagination. Eddie had felt it too. And she wouldn't have to find out what it was on her own.

But that didn't mean it would be safe.

Chapter 9

When Gwen got back to the house, she looked through the kitchen window. Her aunt was stirring something on the cooker. She knocked gently on the glass.

Aunt Tiny opened it an inch.

"You can bring Boo in now, Gwen. They will have to meet eventually. Might as well see what happens over dinner when we can throw them a few scraps to keep them quiet."

Gwen turned round to look at the dog. He sat, tongue lolling, waiting to be let in.

"Now Boo, we have a visitor," she said. "Be nice to her. She isn't going to hurt you, if you don't hurt her."

Which was not necessarily true, but assuming the best of someone had always been her father's advice.

After barely a minute together, Cleo was on top of the piano, her fur standing on end, hissing at Boo, who had his paws on the keys and was barking furiously.

Aunt Tiny stood in the parlour doorway.

"Take Boo into the kitchen. We'll shut this door and let the cat calm down. Then maybe they will make friends later."

Over the dinner of stewed lamb and potatoes, Boo wouldn't stop scratching at the door, desperate to find the cat.

Aunt Tiny sighed and pushed her last potato around her plate to get the remains of the gravy.

"What do you think we should do, Gwen? Do you have any experience of cats?"

Gwen looked up in surprise. At home no one ever asked her advice.

"No. Mummy doesn't like animals. She wouldn't let us keep any."

"You are absolutely right, she was scared of them. How could I forget? But you like animals, and you are good with them and not afraid. How did that happen?"

"Daddy used to take me to the zoo most Saturday mornings when I was little."

He'd enjoyed seeing the animals. It had made him feel calm and happy. They'd both liked the mischievous monkeys particularly. Afterwards they'd go to one of the pavilions in the park for a cup of tea in his case, and a glass of milk and a bun in hers. But when he became unwell, all that had stopped. Nothing had made him feel calm any more. And then one of the worst things had happened.

"That must have been lovely," Aunt Tiny said. She placed her knife and fork carefully together on the plate. "We should get a letter from your mother tomorrow, or the next day if not. Perhaps she'll have more news of your father."

Gwen had stopped eating. Her stomach felt unsteady. Boo left his pawing of the door and lay down under the table at her feet.

"Can I give the rest to Boo?" Gwen asked, picking up her plate.

"Yes, put it in his bowl though. We don't want him getting ideas above his station."

They washed up together in silence until Gwen suddenly had a thought.

"Where is Cleopatra going to do her business if she isn't let outside?"

Aunt Tiny turned to look at her.

"My goodness! I completely forgot. We need to make her a tray with sand in it." Aunt Tiny shook the water off her hands. "Come on, we will do it together. There is a patch of sandy soil in the field by the road."

They went digging in the side of the bank near the road with a spade and a trowel. When they had filled a bucket, they took turns dragging it back to the house.

An old cardboard box was found and cut down to a low tray with a sharp knife. Then they tipped the sand in.

"Where should we put it?" Aunt Tiny asked, wiping her hands on her apron.

"You could put it in my room. I don't mind." Gwen said, eagerly. "Cleo was sitting on my pillow earlier." Gwen could picture the cat sleeping on her pillow by her head every night, and lulling her to sleep with loud purring. Perhaps that would stop the nightmares.

Aunt Tiny put her hands on her hips.

"You know, Gwendoline? You and I are going to get on just fine. Your room it is. But if it is too messy or smelly, we'll move it to the larder."

Rather than the peaceful purring presence on her pillow that Gwen had hoped for, the cat spent most of the night meowing at the closed door and jumping on and off the bed.

Gwen eventually let her out, put the pillow over her ear and the covers over her face and did not wake up until well after nine. When she came yawning into the kitchen, it was empty. Her aunt was in the larder mixing something in a bowl, to judge by the sound. An opened letter from her mother was propped up next to the jug of milk on the kitchen table. There was no sign of the dog.

Gwen poured milk into the saucer for the cat who was standing meaningfully over it. She lapped until it was all gone and rubbed herself against Gwen's legs, meowing for more.

Her aunt came into the kitchen, her hands sticky with dough.

"Good morning, I suspect you had a disturbed night with the queen of cats?"

"I think she will settle down. Moving house has upset her," Gwen said. Even with all the noise and disruption, it was good having Cleo or Boo in the room with her. So much better than her cold and silent bedroom at home, with the empty space where Hugh's bed and Hugh's laughter used to be.

Her aunt nodded and reached up for a tin on the shelf.

"I've put Boo in my studio, just for now. Here, open these sardines for her. I'm sure she'll like them."

Cleo certainly did.

"May I read the letter?"

"Yes, of course. I'll be outside."

Gwen sat down with a glass of milk and took the thin envelope between her fingers. It was addressed to both of them with her mother's precise, sloping hand.

Despite all her effort, Gwen's own handwriting was large and messy by comparison. Her mother was also good at sketching faces, but she hadn't drawn anything since Hugh's death except diagrams of guns at the factory. Gwen unfolded the single sheet of paper.

'Dear Eglantine and Gwendoline,
What a lot of syllables you have between your two names, dear ones! They nearly took up all of a line on this paper.

I miss you very much, Gwen, and hope you are being good for your aunt. I also hope you were neat and well presented when you went to church. Perhaps you will write to me and tell me what the church was like?

Here there is not much to report. I have been working extra hours at the factory. It is taking longer and longer to get to Small Heath because some of the roads are damaged. Your father is due to come home for a visit soon. He will be so sad that you are not here, but also happy that you are safe. He writes that he is enjoying the work they have given him in the farm near the hospital. He is cleaning out the horses. He always liked being with animals. I have told him your address, and he promises to write to you soon.'

The rest of the letter was about sending money to Aunt Tiny for the school equipment. Gwen put the letter down and wiped her eyes. Her father was going to be at home, and she would not be there. If he came to Netherwood, he could help her with the pony and the chickens. They could go to Quarry Wood and investigate the strange thing in the yew tree together. It would not be frightening with him beside her. If he was feeling better, he would play the piano, and she would sing. It would help him; she knew it would.

But she did not have his address to suggest the plan. And she also knew her mother would not be happy if he was here, not with her in the city.

Gwen got up from the table and went to the window. Leaves were being blown off the trees by a strong wind. This kind of weather made horses nervous, she remembered. Brushing Hilda could wait until the weather settled in the afternoon, but seeing to the chickens could not. There were puddles in the yard so Gwen put on the old boots that had belonged to one of the boys and trudged out to the henhouse, wondering if Eddie would go with her to the Quarry Wood that day or make an excuse when they met by the stream.

But Eddie didn't come at all and the weather continued to be stormy. Gwen waited by the stream for almost an hour, hunched over the bridge railing, watching Boo getting wetter and wetter while water dripped from the edge of her coat. Eventually she dragged herself home, found the old book and slid into bed to read. Cleopatra had curled up on the bottom of the bed, just too far for Gwen to reach with her toes. She was licking her paws with a bright pink tongue.

Gwen turned the pages to chapter seven to read about fairies. She skimmed through some rather long descriptions of their favoured places.

The white thorn is one of the trees most in favour with the small people [the fairies]; and both in Brittany and in some parts of Ireland it is held unsafe to gather even a leaf from certain old and solitary thorns which grow in sheltered hollows of the moorland, and are the fairies' trysting places. But no evil ghost dares to approach the white thorn.

And a bit further down the page:

A Celtic hairy wood-demon was called 'Dus', hence our modern 'the Deuce.'

Gwen sighed. It wasn't a wood-demon that was up in that tree. These beliefs were just the way people explained unknown natural things. There were plenty of real things, like bombs, to be afraid of. The frightening shadow would disappear if she faced it. There would be some perfectly sensible explanation. It was silly to be afraid of a tree.

She got up and went to the window. The sun had come out, and the sky was almost entirely blue. Her aunt would be in her studio for a few more hours. She could go up to the wood and be back before tea.

Gwen made sure that the dog and cat were shut in separate rooms, filled a bottle with water and pushed in the stopper. The moon was already up, a pale scrap of whiteness in the eastern sky above the wood.

Then she went up the drive and closed the gate behind her.

There was something about the light that seemed to pick out every leaf in the hedge, every darkening blackberry. Even as she went past the farm with its milk cans by the muddy track, the long grasses of the verge were shining golden-green fronds. Somewhere someone was hammering a plank of wood. The echo of it sounded from the barn walls.

Soon Gwen was at the turning into the wood. She paused a moment to catch her breath after the hill and looked back down at the valley. The sun was two hand widths from setting, and the only visible clouds were gathered on the distant hills.

No one would miss her.

She had plenty of time.

Gwen went slowly along the path between the trees, walking as quietly as possible, her chest tightening around each breath. A sudden movement overhead made her start. A large black bird was moving from one foot to another, holding a two-pronged twig in its thick beak. The raven cocked its head at her, croaked loudly, flexed its dark scaly legs and pushed off, flying deeper into the wood.

Gwen's hands were damp although the day was cool. She rubbed them on her skirt and took a deep breath. It felt different being there on her own – like there were things just out of sight watching her. There were so many hiding places. Some of the tree trunks were surrounded by spurs of low branches, like spikey, wizened beards. Other trees were encircled by thick ropes of ivy. In the green pasture just beyond the trees, a hare was dodging through the tall grass.

There was a newly fallen tree on the path. Gwen stepped over it cautiously. Its roots stuck out from the thin soil over white stone. It must have fallen in the wind only hours before.

Gwen looked at the gash in the ground. On the way back she would look for a fresh fossil in there to show Eddie. Proof she had gone on her own.

Soon she was at the entrance to the gully. The gap where Eddie had hacked out the lump of fossil stone looked like a dark eye – or a mouth. Gwen reached out tentatively and put her hand inside. It was damp and cool. She rubbed the crumbly bits of stone between her fingers. The remains of a seabed from millions of years ago, and here she was touching it, while tractors rumbled away below and somewhere people were building planes and guns. And they'd all come from these small, simple creatures.

She put the bottle of water down by the trunk of the tall holly tree and turned her back on the gully. This was not why she had come. The sooner she went, the sooner it would be done.

Gwen started down the path, wondering where to start climbing towards the yew tree glade. After a little while she noticed a faint track of broken plant stems on the hillside. It could be the place where she and Eddie had run pell-mell down the hill, chasing Boo after he had run away from the yew tree. She went up carefully over lumps of rock and fallen branches with birdsong all around her until she reached the top.

The glade looked different. Perhaps it was the low sun. It gleamed on the elder berries, giving them a metallic sheen. Rather than running straight across the glade, Gwen began picking her way around its circumference, from tree to tree, heading towards the yew.

She stopped when she was about ten yards away from its thick trunk, just outside the reach of its branches, and looked all around. There was nothing above or beside her. A slight breeze was moving the elder leaves. Somewhere in the distance, perhaps in the quarry, an engine coughed.

She stepped forward quickly and went up to the trunk, not touching it. Fallen red berries stuck to her shoes. The hair on the back of her neck was standing up, but she forced herself to look up into its branches.

The centre of the yew was almost flat where the three main branches emerged. It looked like a seat – or a throne. But there was nothing else there. No otherworldly creature. No pale cold arm reaching down with long, rigid fingers, just reddish brown branches and the thick curtains of dark green needles.

"Hello," she called, her voice high and brittle.

A jay's call of alarm sounded behind her. She counted to ten under her breath, her hands clenched at her sides. Then she looked up into the heart of the tree again.

Still nothing.

But the backs of her hands were pricking like before, and she couldn't stop her feet from running back the way she'd come, around the glade, down the hill and all the way to the gully.

She sank to the ground by the holly tree, breathing hard. Tears began streaming from her eyes, falling on the soil. She covered her face with her hands. It was too much. She was going mad just like her father. Imagining scary things. Turning strange. She would soon be locked away, just like him. Then her mother would have lost both her children, and Gwen would be all alone, not allowed visitors or pets.

The sobbing took a long time to stop, but eventually she rested her head on her knees and took a deep shuddering breath, glad that Eddie was not there to see her humiliated, covered in tears and snot. She felt for her handkerchief in her pocket, wiped her eyes and blew her nose. Her throat was sore and dry.

Gwen turned to reach for the water bottle.

Next to it was an upright figure, not much bigger than a doll. Its face was old and wizened, with the shine of polished, fine-grained wood. The nose was round and bright red. Its eyes were black, and its upper body was covered in glossy holly leaves. Its hands were three-pronged green twigs. Around it, the air moved in visible waves, like heat haze. It took a step towards her, and the gash in the face where a mouth should be opened.

"What a noise," it said, sounding like two branches rubbing against one another. "Worse than a banshee, you are."

Chapter 10

Gwen sat with her arm still stretched out towards the water bottle, her mouth hanging open, frozen.

"Not so noisy now, are you, child?" the tiny wooden creature said.

He looked at her, and the black eyes gleamed a little. The sound he made was a screeching chuckle. He sat down facing her.

"Never seen one before, I'm guessing." He nodded his head and snapped his twig fingers. Gwen took a gasp of breath. "Never seen a tree spirit before, have you?" he creaked.

Gwen shook her head and lowered her trembling hand.

"Give us a drink then. I've tasted your tears, now I want some fresh water."

Gwen looked at him with wide eyes.

"You want –" she managed, reaching again for the bottle.

"Yes, yes. I thought human people were meant to be clever."

Gwen kept her eyes on the creature, while her fingers struggled to pull the stopper. When it finally popped, she held the bottle out to him, wordlessly.

"Not me, silly child. My tree of course! Pour it down there," he said, pointing at the rise of roots at the base of the holly.

The water glugged onto the stony soil, sinking in quickly. The creature sighed in a satisfied way and waved his twiggy arms in the air.

"Summer. We are always thirsty in summer." He settled back down, his leaves rustling against one another.

"What are you?" Gwen whispered. "Where do you come from?"

The creature made the same chuckling sound as before, his eyes narrowing and cracks appearing in the wood of his face.

"I am Gelyn. A tree spirit. And this holly tree you have been weeping under is my home."

Gwen rubbed her eyes and gave her head a violent shake. When she opened her eyes again, the creature was still there.

"I am going mad," she whispered.

"You sounded like a demented pixie earlier. But if you think that you have lost your mind because you are seeing a tree spirit, you are wrong. Many people have seen us over the centuries. You are not the first."

"But why can I see you?" she cried.

The creature didn't say anything. He put his splayed twig hands on the ground and closed its eyes. After a few moments he opened them.

"You came here five sunsets ago?"

Gwen nodded.

"And something made you come back. Something you saw?"

Gwen's throat was closed and tight. She nodded again.

"Where did you see it?"

"In the old yew tree," Gwen said, pointing.

The creature shook his head slowly from side to side.

"Well, what do you expect? If you see one, you must see them all."

"What do you mean?" Gwen cried. "What did I see?"

"In the case of the yew, that is slightly different. The yew is the seat of the lords and ladies of the wood. Elves, to you. I suppose you saw one of them. One of them who was – how would you understand it? Perhaps 'hunting' is the best description. It was open to view because you stepped into its aura. The coldness. Brave of you." He nodded, a little grudgingly. "But now you will be able to see all the elves and the other spirits of this wood."

Gwen sat on her trembling hands and leaned towards the holly spirit.

"So there was a thing in the yew tree that was trying to catch Boo?"

"Who?"

"My dog." She shook her head. "My aunt's dog. His name is Boo."

"That is an odd name for an animal," the creature commented. "But you are right. Elves like causing mischief for people, leading them astray. It amuses them." The tree spirit fixed its eyes on Gwen's. "If you had not gone to the tree at that moment and touched the dog, it would have been taken."

"Taken where?" Gwen breathed.

The holly creature tapped the ground with one of his twiggy fingers.

"Below." His expression challenged her to ask more.

Gwen laughed nervously. She got up.

"I must be having a dream." She stamped her feet and tugged on her plaits until her scalp hurt.

The creature looked at her crossly.

"That won't help. Once you've seen one, you can't help seeing us all. I told you." He stood up and walked towards his tree. "Most people consider it an honour."

He went over to the trunk, his twig fingers outstretched.

"Wait, don't go!" Gwen cried. "I have so many things to ask you!" The holly creature paused, his head cocked haughtily. "I'm very glad to see you. You are wonderful," Gwen went on.

The creature twitched his leaves and turned a little towards her.

"I'm one of the oldest of all the spirits," he said, gloatingly.

"You must be very wise," Gwen tried. "You probably know everything about this wood."

He held his head proudly.

"Only Oak is older. But he is too sleepy to come out, except if the right rituals are observed. You are lucky that you chose to sit under my tree first, and not an Elder. They are on the side of the elves. They would have let them take you as well as the dog."

"Do you mean the trees around the glade?"

"Some trees are used by the lords and ladies and enjoy the attention. Their flowers and berries can tempt people. And sometimes, they are led away," he said.

Gwen shivered. She stared at the remarkable creature. He was looking restless.

"Please tell me your name again."

"Gelyn. If you are in dire need, you can touch any holly, say my name and I will come. If you wish simply to talk to me, bring me an offering, but do not treat me like a servant. I have important work and speaking to you will distract me from it. There is much unseen by you that goes on underground."

"I won't. I promise," Gwen said sincerely. "Do you have to go now?"

"I might stay a little longer," the holly creature conceded. "You brought me a good offering." He looked meaningfully at the empty water bottle and sat down on a stone.

"Have there been others who could see you?"

Gelyn looked at her with a crafty expression.

"I think you already know the answer to that. There has only been one in the past hundred years. It has been a sad time. Machines and motors, but few who are willing to understand the trees." He sighed. "He knew our kind from his home country, but now the friend who knew my name is gone."

"Anders," Gwen whispered. "Of course."

"He was close to Ash. Ash was the tree he spoke to first."

Gwen tried to recall the painting in the hall where Anders had recorded his friends of the wood. She would have to study it closely when she got back.

"Are there tree spirits in every forest? Like down in the woods by the house?" But she thought she also knew the answer to that before the little creature shook his head.

"No, there are very few places left for us. We can only exist where there is one of each of the ancient trees: Oak and Holly, Thorn and Ash. The ground must remain undisturbed, the trees left to grow tall and thick. And if there is also an ancient Yew, then the elves will come."

"But this is only a small wood. In the valley, there are many more trees," Gwen said pointing towards Netherwood Coppice.

"But in the valley the ground is not so steep, so the men are coming every few years with their axes and saws, their hooks and boots. This may be small but it is ancient, one of the last pieces of the ancient forest that once lay thick across this land. Thousands of years ago, the men started chopping it down to make their dwellings and their fires, driving us out." The holly creature grimaced. "And if the people over the ridge with their drills have their way, this will all be gone too, and we will go with the trees, burnt up in a fire or turned into a chair for your human bottoms."

"They are going to cut down the wood?" Gwen said horrified. "They can't!"

The little creature seemed satisfied.

"You are another friend. I knew it."

He was looking smug, his little arms crossed on his leafy chest.

"Was that a test?" she asked. "Did you just say that to see how I would react?"

Gelyn looked straight into her eyes.

"They will try to cut it down, one day." In his eyes, she seemed to see the yew bleeding from many cuts around its base. "Maybe soon, maybe not. And when they do, you may not be able to stop them."

"There would be a way," she said, her hands clenched in her lap.

"As soon as men discover how to make money out of land, they stop caring for the trees, or for anything else."

"My aunt said the owner of the quarry is very greedy. Does he come into the wood?"

The creature rustled his leaves as if shivering.

"He walked here years ago. One day, perhaps, he will be elf-led and not walk out," Gelyn said with a smirk.

Gwen remembered the way Boo had been pawing at the tree, oblivious of anything around him.

"Is that what happened to my dog? Was he elf-led?"

"No." Gelyn shook his head. "They wanted to take him into their realm. They are fascinated by creatures that are loved because they feel nothing like that themselves. The more a creature is valued by people, the more the elves will want to take it. It is a curiosity for them, and an entertainment. They watch the people searching and find it amusing. Then maybe one day they let it go, and the people are amazed that it comes back years later. But for the dog or cat or child that was taken, it felt like only a few days." The holly creature seemed to relish this story, then seeing Gwen's shocked face he added: "But they have not taken any children for years. They don't like loud men poking around in the wood."

Gwen's stomach turned. Children taken from their parents just for the amusement of the elves? They must be very cruel to take pleasure in such sadness. She dragged her attention back to the holly creature who was still speaking in his squeaky, scraping voice.

"What would happen to that greedy quarryman would be quite different. They wouldn't want him in their realm, as there is no one who loves him to search for him, so they would simply confuse," Gelyn said loftily. "In other places they might lead him into a bog or a lake. Here they could make him climb a very tall tree, or perhaps lead him in a dance so that he fell off the cliffs of his own quarry."

"But he would die if he fell," Gwen said in a small voice.

The creature turned and looked at her squarely.

"Yes, but all people die. Don't they, Gwen. You know that." He was no longer smiling. His eyes bored into hers, and, as if watching a coloured newsreel, she saw her brother, Hugh, in his bed, blue-lipped and still, his eyes open and unseeing, her mother crying on her knees by his side. The scene changed and she was looking at the burnt and flattened remains of Mrs Usher's house at number 4, Hart Road, and feeling the raw pain of the cut on her palm. The images changed again and a grey-faced man who must be Anders was lying flat on his back by a pile of firewood.

"Stop it!" Gwen cried, scrambling to her feet, tears blurring her vision. "What are you doing? How did you make me see them?"

"I see what is in the heart. You love your brother although he is gone. You also care for the memory of the old woman and my dear friend whom you call Anders. Those who live on in your heart do not die. But if a man lives only for money, who will mourn him if he dies? And if his death saves the forest, wouldn't that be for the best?"

Gwen pressed her fists into her eyes.

"I don't know! I don't want anyone to die. I just want my family to be safe, and you and the trees.

Why do we have to have wars? Why can't we all be safe?" she shouted.

"Hey, what are you shouting for?" a voice said behind her. "You're frightening the birds!"

She opened her eyes to see Eddie standing at the bottom of the gully looking up towards her, his face concerned, the satchel slung over his shoulder. Behind him a flock of black ravens streamed out of the wood.

Gwen looked all around her, but the holly creature had disappeared.

Chapter 11

Eddie took a couple of steps towards her.

"What's happened? You look like you've seen a ghost." He tipped his head to one side. "Gwen, what's wrong?"

Gwen fumbled for her handkerchief, turned away from him and blew her nose. Her whole body was trembling.

"I'm all right," she said, reaching for the bottle of water by the tree trunk. It was empty. She'd forgotten that she'd poured it into the roots of the holly tree. But that meant she had not been dreaming. She looked around the gully, but there was still no sign of the creature. "Do you have anything to drink? I'm so thirsty."

"Yes, I've brought some elderflower cordial." He was still looking at her with a wary expression. She sat down on a log and shoved her hankie into her pocket.

"Hey, why did you come up here on your own? I told you yesterday that I'd come with you." Eddie lowered his satchel to the ground and looked around the gully following her eyes. "Something scared you?"

"It was just a badger," she said without thinking. "I was sitting under the tree and it came very close to me."

"Really? They don't usually come out so early. It's at least an hour until sunset. That's strange." He had unstrapped the satchel and was taking out a bevelled glass bottle.

"Yes, and then it got frightened and ran away, and that's when you must have heard me shouting," Gwen explained, in a strange flat voice.

"Enough to wake the dead. I thought a German soldier had parachuted into the wood, and you were telling him off." He held out the bottle. "Here, have some of this. My mum makes it."

"What did you say it was?" Gwen asked, taking the bottle suspiciously.

"Elderflower cordial, made with elderflowers. It's diluted with water," he said very slowly. "Haven't you ever had that?"

"No thank you," she said holding the bottle away from her. Drinking elder seemed foolish, considering what Gelyn had told her.

"Why?"

"I'm not thirsty any more."

"You are completely barmy," Eddie said, shaking his head and grabbing the bottle out of her hand. "It's lovely," he swigged it, and when he lowered the bottle, half was gone. "By the way, I met your crazy cat, Cleopatra. She is chasing your dog round the house until it is a quivering wreck." He looked down at her, wrinkling his brow. "Do you know you have holly leaves in your hair?"

She put her hands up to her head. Prickly leaves were trapped in the folds of her plaits.

"I can't decide if you look more like a wood fairy or a scarecrow!" he chortled.

Gwen stood up, still shaking.

"I'm going home. Got to check on the dog and cat," she muttered and ran past him onto the path.

"Hey, what about going to the yew tree?" he shouted after her.

"There's nothing there!" Gwen replied, not turning round.

After a while she heard him following her.

"Slow down! You don't need to run all the way." He put his hand on her shoulder. "Gwen, what happened back there? You are even stranger than usual."

She slowed but kept moving.

"Nothing happened. There is nothing there, and I'm fine," she insisted. After a few strides she added: "You can help me with the pony when we get back."

"Just what I need, another job," he muttered.

A few more paces.

"Listen, if something did happen, you can tell me. I won't tell anyone else."

She turned at that.

"What do you mean?"

"I won't tell anyone at school. They wouldn't understand. They live in the town. They don't know about the woods."

"What about the woods?"

Eddie looked around him. A squirrel was running up the trunk of an ash tree. Small birds were chirruping in the thicket on the edge of the field. And again, if she paid attention, the sounds would almost turn into words.

"These woods, well – they have a peculiar feeling," he said, slowly. "It's hard to describe."

She waited, hoping that somehow he already knew, and she wouldn't have to keep this secret all alone.

"It feels different somehow, not like other places," he said. "Maybe it wasn't a good idea for you to come on your own." He looked up at the overarching branches. "Maybe I shouldn't have brought you at all."

She shook her head.

"Why wasn't it a good idea?" she whispered.

He sighed deeply, as if resigned to something.

"The Greencoats are said to live here. My grandfather used to talk about them. You have to watch out for their places; they cause all kinds of trouble."

Gwen's stomach flipped over. She gripped her skirt in both fists.

"What are Greencoats?"

"I don't know, some kind of fairy or something. It's just a silly story," he said without conviction.

She stared at him, wavering.

"What do they do?"

"Steal things, mainly. Sometimes they trick people. Make them do things."

Gwen turned away.

"It's getting late. Let's go home."

And she set off, walking quickly with Eddie's footsteps behind her, unable to speak any more for all the thoughts crowding her mind.

They brushed the pony in complete silence, and then Eddie left, striding across the field towards the sinking sun.

Aunt Tiny was already in the kitchen, stirring onions and butter in an iron pan on the cooker. The smell made Gwen's stomach rumble immediately.

"Hello Gwen." Her aunt half-turned, her arm still stirring. "You've been out a long time. Did Eddie find you?"

Boo came racing into the kitchen and nuzzled her hand. She knelt down and put both arms around his neck. He licked the side of her face.

"Yes, he's gone home now."

"I saw him from my studio window looking everywhere for you." Aunt Tiny's voice was cheerful, but there was some other emotion in it. It reminded Gwen of her mother.

"Where did you go?"

"Just up to find fossils," Gwen said, hoping her own voice sounded normal. Boo had flopped on the floor and rolled on his back. She gave his belly a good scratch.

"Ah. I thought so." Aunt Tiny stirred the onions several times before continuing. "It's not a good idea to be going that far on your own, darling. Especially with the quarry so near, and the war –" Her voice petered out. "It's fine to go with Eddie, though."

Gwen felt tears starting in her eyes.

"But I like it in the wood, and I haven't seen any other people there at all!"

"Yes, it is lovely there, I know. But your mother has asked me to look after you," Aunt Tiny said, turning to look straight at Gwen for the first time, "and I would be happier if you didn't go so far on your own." She came towards Gwen. "Darling, are you feeling ill? You look very pale."

Gwen turned her face away.

"I'm fine, just hungry. May I have a cup of tea please, Auntie?"

"Of course, there's water in the kettle." But Aunt Tiny did not move back to the cooker. She stood quite still looking at Gwen, absentmindedly wiping her hands on her apron. "Gwen –"

Boo suddenly wriggled himself onto his feet and raced out of the kitchen. The cat had come out of the larder. Gwen took advantage of the disruption to change the subject.

Gwen did feel better after the cup of tea. She peeled potatoes and chopped carrots, and, after a few mouthfuls of sausage, the tremors in her chest completely stopped. But she had to force herself to answer her aunt's attempts at conversation. All she wanted to do was go to the stairway and study the painting by Anders. He had known the ash tree. It would certainly be there. And she thought she remembered seeing the holly.

"Did you bring any fossils back from the wood?" her aunt was asking.

"No, we didn't find any good ones," Gwen lied.

Aunt Tiny frowned a little.

"That wood used to be called Ravenshaw, before the quarry came," she said thoughtfully. "So the ravens that nest in the quarry cliff must have had other nesting places in those days. Did you see many ravens?" Aunt Tiny was looking at her intently, her carrot-laden fork in mid-air, forgotten.

"Yes, they fly around a bit," Gwen said uncomfortably.

"Do you know the story about Odin's ravens?"

Gwen shook her head.

"Who is Odin?"

"He is the King of the Norse gods. Anders told me about him and all the other Scandinavian gods. They believe in a huge world tree, a great ash or yew, there is some disagreement about that, and Odin was sacrificed on it."

"Like Jesus on the cross?" Gwen asked.

"Hmm, maybe." Aunt Tiny noticed the fork, put it in her mouth, and chewed the carrot slowly. "But the tree was more than that. It was where the gods resided and held their courts each day. It might be seen as more of a ladder to different worlds. But in any event, Odin in the world tree has two ravens that sit on his shoulders. He sends them out, and they fly over the world and bring back news of the past and the future." She was looking into the middle distance, as if remembering something herself. "And they have the power of speech."

Gwen shivered a little.

"The raven's voice is very like a human child, maybe that is why," Aunt Tiny was saying.

"Mmmm," Gwen said. She pushed her knife and fork together carefully. "I'm feeling very tired, Auntie. May I wash my plate and go to bed?"

Gwen hoped Aunt Tiny would stay in the kitchen so that she could examine the painting closely without having to answer any more questions. But her aunt's concern for her meant she followed her up the stairs, came into her room and sat on the edge of the bed to check her temperature.

"You don't seem to have a fever," she said, pressing the back of her hand to Gwen's forehead. "But you certainly don't look quite right." She picked up Gwen's hand where it lay on the coverlet, examined the scar, and then gave it a warm squeeze. "Did you and Eddie have an argument?"

"No," Gwen said firmly. "I think I'm just tired from the cat waking me up at night. Could we put the sand box in the larder instead?"

"Of course. I'll take it now, and if you keep your door shut, she won't come in and bother you."

Gwen lay very still in bed, but there was no danger of her falling asleep. Every minute she had spent with Gelyn went through her head over and over again, and half the time she was convinced that she was indeed mad and had imagined it all, and then she would remind herself of the water, of the holly leaves, and the legend of the Greencoats, as Eddie called them. Known to be troublemakers by those who had always lived here near the wood.

Eventually the door of Aunt Tiny's bedroom closed with a loud click. Amongst the sounds of her getting ready for bed, Gwen struck a match and lit the candle on the bedside table.

She would wait for silence and then count to five hundred. By then her aunt should be fully asleep.

Gwen went as quietly as possible across the floorboards to the door. A breeze in the hallway made her candle gutter alarmingly. She shielded it with her hand and went slowly one foot at a time down the stairs, hoping that Boo was fast asleep in Aunt Tiny's room and wouldn't notice.

Gwen descended the last staircase where the painting hung, halfway down on the inside wall. She held the candle high and peered at it. The flickering of the flame made the figures shift and sway. Gwen blinked her eyes, tired from staying awake, and looked again.

In the centre there was a tall smooth-trunked ash tree. In the process of coming out of a split in the bark was the figure of an elegant young spirit, lime-green like spring leaves, its leafy arms reaching out, all willowy, drooping and beautiful.

To the right of it was the massive oak tree. A serious, rugged spirit stood by it, arms stretched up, staring out at the viewer.

On the other side, more closely painted, was a hawthorn half-covered in blossom and half with bright red haws, and the spirit of it was sharp and frosty, authoritative and distant. Finally at the far edge of the painting was the holly. He was small and close to the ground, his little red nose barely visible, the crack of a grin on his tiny face. It was quite obviously a portrait of Gelyn.

Gwen stepped back and looked at the whole of the painting. The background was dark and full of forest, but she thought she saw birds against the flashes of evening sky. Where was the yew? Had he chosen not to paint it at all? Had he known the elves or only the tree spirits?

She had leaned in to look once more, when she noticed a faint sound. It was growing quickly louder. She blew out the candle and ran up the stairs. They trembled under her feet. She reached her bedroom window as one flew almost over the house in a roar of thudding metal and air.

She counted the lights, leaning out into the night, her hands numb on the window frame.

Twenty-three bombers heading east. More than ever before.

Aunt Tiny found Gwen almost falling out of the window as the last of the planes went over, and took her gently downstairs to her bedroom.

"You don't want to be alone when this is happening and neither do I," she said, sliding into the other side of the bed. "We will just keep each other company and pray that the anti-aircraft guns pick them all off before they do their terrible business."

Gwen lay still, listening to her aunt's breathing. She wasn't falling asleep either.

"Aunt Tiny?"

"Yes?"

"Have you ever heard of Greencoats?"

Her aunt shifted in bed and sat up against the pillows.

"Yes, I have. They are mischievous woodland spirits, I believe. Where did you hear about them? Was it Eddie?"

Gwen nodded.

"Has he been frightening you with tales of children being led astray in the wood?" Aunt Tiny asked, looking sideways at Gwen, her tone quite cross. "He ought to know better."

"No, he didn't. He just mentioned them in passing, that's all."

Aunt Tiny was quiet for a bit.

"Eddie used to listen to Anders for hours. Anders used to pay him for carrying logs and other errands. It gave Anders an excuse to tell the stories of Denmark after his own boys got too old and started leaving home. They enjoyed each other's company, I think." She pulled the covers a little higher. "Eddie is a good lad. He is more sensible than most of the boys you will come across at that school. I have a high opinion of him. But," Aunt Tiny patted Gwen's shoulder "don't take all his tales as true. There are lots of superstitious people in the countryside, and it's fun for them to try out their hobgoblins on city folk."

"Yes, Auntie."

Aunt Tiny sighed.

"I'm sorry things have been so sad for you. I'm also sorry that we have only just got to know each other." She patted Gwen's shoulder again. "I hope you will have a good time staying here. I think you are a lovely girl."

Gwen felt like crying. She knew she should turn and hug her aunt, but there were too many things she was trying to keep inside, and if she got close to Aunt Tiny, they would all come spilling out in a great big mess.

"It's nice here," she said in a very quiet voice. "I'm glad I came."

"I'm very pleased to hear it," her aunt said. In the silence afterwards, they both sat up. The familiar rumble of aircraft was coming from the other side of the house.

"We won't watch, Gwen. Come with me and we will hide under the bed. Sometimes they drop bombs on the way back, just to save the weight." She pulled Gwen off the bed and they rolled under it into a layer of dust.

Gwen tried to count the planes going by, but the sound was muffled and continuous.

"We will hear on the wireless tomorrow how many were shot down," Aunt Tiny whispered. In that darkness, under the bed next to her aunt, Gwen had a strange feeling of peace, as if a warm and heavy blanket of protection was comforting her. Her limbs were heavy with exhaustion. Eventually Aunt Tiny sneezed and rolled over.

"I think they've gone now," she said. "Let's dust ourselves off and try to get some sleep."

They found Boo hiding under a small desk in the parlour and brought him upstairs. He slept in a warm lump between them, occasionally waking up and licking Gwen's ear.

Chapter 12

When Gwen woke, Aunt Tiny was already up and gone, the dog as well. She padded downstairs, still in her nightie. She'd not had any strange dreams, and her head felt clear for the first time in many days. Gwen decided that she was not going to allow herself to think about the wood and what had happened there yet. First she must find out about the bomb damage.

She looked out of the kitchen window. It was a bright, dry day. A pair of swallows dipped down in a shaft of sunlight, their wings glistening black and brown, then swerved over the henhouse and away. Her aunt was just coming out of her studio. She crossed the yard and came through the door, followed by the dog.

"I just missed the first broadcast," she said, wiping her feet on the mat. "There'll be another at nine."

Gwen rushed upstairs to get dressed, and they had a quick breakfast. Her heart started beating fast as they approached the studio together. She hadn't been allowed in before, and perhaps wouldn't be again. And more importantly, what would the wireless news say about Birmingham, if anything?

Aunt Tiny fished a key out of her skirt pocket and turned it in the lock, but stopped on the threshold, the door only open a crack.

"Gwen, I'm sure you understand that you mustn't touch anything in here. Some of the work is in a very fragile state." Her aunt's gaze held her own. "This is my main source of income, so you must be very careful with it."

"I won't touch, Auntie. I promise." Gwen had a sudden question. "But doesn't Boo make a mess when he comes in?"

Aunt Tiny smiled a little and shook her head.

"I told you. Anders sent him. He's a very wise dog and always lies well out of the way." She opened the door and stepped through. "But we will never, ever let that troublesome cat in here, will we? I'm beginning to think we should pop her on a bus and send her to town."

The studio was colder than the house. A large white sink stood against the far wall. Charcoal sketches of numerous faces and profiles papered the walls. There were stands in front of each of the four windows, but they were covered in wet muslin cloths so it was impossible to see what was underneath. They looked like four rather grubby ghosts.

Gwen stood in the middle of the room, her arms folded so that she wouldn't knock against anything. The wireless in the far corner was very old. Her aunt bent down to turn it on, and it made several loud pops before a fragment of faint music emerged. Aunt Tiny turned a large black knob and, after a moment, a man's voice began:

"This is the BBC Home Service. The time is nine o'clock. Here is the news and this is Bruce Belfrage reading it."

But they had to wait and wait, through reports of British air raids in Africa, the recent naval success in the Mediterranean, the comment on news from Romania, and finally right at the end:

"German bombers attacking a Midlands town last night were brought down by anti-aircraft fire in large numbers. A large dock was also targeted and defended. Across the region, more than twelve planes were damaged or destroyed. The area is defiant, as is London, and the people of the Midlands are working harder than ever for the war effort. Now we join Vera Lynn with 'A Nightingale sang in Berkeley Square.'"

A woman's strong singing voice filled the room.

"But they didn't tell us anything!" Gwen complained. "They didn't say where the bombs were dropped."

"No," Aunt Tiny said thoughtfully, switching off the wireless.

In the sudden silence, they could hear Boo scratching at the door. Gwen let him in.

"I think it is their policy not to broadcast the specific places that have been damaged now. I have noticed that they are not saying half what they used to. But twelve planes is a good number."

"If it's true," Gwen said, hugging herself. "They might just be trying to make everyone feel better and pretend we are winning." She noticed the bitter tone of her words and looked over at her aunt.

"We will have to wait for a letter from your mother to find out," Aunt Tiny said, looking out of a window as if hoping for a pigeon to fly in with a message tied to its leg.

"What if –" but Gwen couldn't ask the rest of her question. It was too awful.

Aunt Tiny went over to one of the covered stands. Either she hadn't heard, or she was ignoring the thing Gwen couldn't voice. No one could tell her what would happen if her mother was already dead and couldn't write. It was war. Would anyone even send them a telegram or get word to her father?

"Come over here, Gwen. I will show you my lovely Anders."

For a moment Gwen was horrified. Was part of Anders' body, his head maybe, under that stained cloth? She shook herself free of the thought and walked over to her aunt.

"I have been working on this since the month after he died." Aunt Tiny gently lifted the cloth away.

Under it was a clay head, about life-size. The top and back of the head were unfinished, thick with stuck-on bits of rough clay. But the face was alive. The mouth was slightly parted. It seemed he was about to speak. Wrinkles creased the skin around the eyes, as if he had often found a reason to smile.

There was the suggestion of a light moustache below a large straight nose. Across one cheek was a mark, like a ragged tear.

Gwen felt her hand reaching out and tucked it back under her other arm. Her aunt was staring at the bust with a fixed expression. She reached out and using her fingernail, she made a line in the clay above his broad forehead, like a sweep of thinning hair.

"What happened to his cheek?" Gwen asked, pointing to the mark.

Aunt Tiny stood back from the portrait head and folded her arms.

"Anders was conscripted into the German army early in the Great War. Do you know what that means?" Aunt Tiny asked, but did not wait for a reply. "His country, Denmark, was neutral, but he lived in the south of the country and was captured and forced to fight on the German side. If he objected to what they made him do, they hurt him." She reached forward again and with the tip of her finger she softened the mark on his cheek. "But luckily he was captured again, quite early on in the war, by the British and put in a camp here. If that had not happened he would have died, either by German hands or their enemies. His life was snatched out of a blazing fire. He loved this country for that, and he always wanted to give back his work and talents as thanks for their decency in time of war."

Aunt Tiny picked up the muslin and took it to the sink. She turned on the tap and soaked the cloth, squeezed it lightly, and stretched it out. Then she walked back with it and placed it gently over the head again.

"I don't know when I will finish it. Perhaps I will continue fiddling with it until I die," she laughed. "It is like having a conversation with him, making it and changing it."

"What about the other ones?" Gwen turned to look at the other stands. "Are they all of Anders?"

"No, my darling," Aunt Tiny said, snapping her fingers for the dog. "They are dearly loved sons who have died in the war. I am making memorials for their families. I won't show you them. They are not ready for anyone's eyes yet." She moved towards the door. "If I hear anything on the news broadcast this afternoon, I will tell you at supper."

She held the door open for Gwen and locked it firmly behind them.

The news bulletins said no more about Birmingham, but a letter from Gwen's mother arrived the following morning. Its very existence was a relief, but the contents were another matter. There was no damage to their home, but the BSA Factory in Small Heath had been bombed. No one had been killed, thank God, but the main rifle barrel production had been destroyed.

The company needed all the staff to work even longer hours to tidy up and get things back into production. Gwen's mother was sorry, but it seemed she wouldn't be able to visit for quite a while.

Aunt Tiny folded the letter and pushed it back in the thin envelope.

"Isn't that good news?" she said with a falsely happy expression. "No harm done!"

Gwen nodded and went into the yard with the excuse of getting her jobs done. She was not stupid. She could tell bad news from terrible news. And this was definitely the former. If they targeted the factory, her mother and all the other people who worked there were also targets.

And the more hours her mother spent there, the more likely she was to die in a bomb blast.

Gwen looked up at the sky. It was bright, bright blue. How could there be planes full of bombs in such a sky? And fire and blood afterwards? What made them want to do it?

She opened the stable door, but Hilda was not there, and nor was the halter. Just as Gwen was about to set off across the meadow to look for the pony, Aunt Tiny put her head out of the kitchen door.

"I forgot to tell you," she called. "I've sold Hilda to a farmer. He came to get her yesterday when you were out with Eddie. We don't use her often enough to make it worth her feed. I'll probably buy her back at the end of the war." Aunt Tiny was still wearing the false smile, as if having to get rid of her pony was the best thing that had ever happened to her, whereas it was obviously another piece of bad news. Aunt Tiny was running out of money.

But at least the arm-aching job of brushing the pony was over.

If anything, they should be getting rid of Cleopatra, who ate her own weight in sardines every day and kept Boo so scared that he'd taken to only coming into the house when Cleo was locked up in the larder. The cat had been let outside for the first time the day before, but had refused to run away. Instead she had concentrated on catching birds and terrorizing the chickens. Aunt Tiny had sighed, said it was early days, and she was sure things would settle down.

Gwen was not. The cat had been the centre of attention at her previous home where she'd ruled the roost. There had been a girl at Gwen's old school like that – a spoilt child who always expected to get her way. Cleopatra was unlikely to suddenly have a change of character. Gwen decided to ask Eddie if they needed a mouser on their farm. Maybe the geese would take her down a peg or two.

She idly wondered where Hilda had gone. Eddie would have told her if it was his father who'd bought the pony. He'd told her a lot of things the day before, about his brothers, who were both bullies, and about the best friend he'd had at school who'd left without a word. Later on Eddie had found out that the boy's family had emigrated to Canada, as they had distant relatives there. He still sounded very sad about it, although it had happened a whole year ago, just before the war started.

It was as if Eddie was a different person since he'd seen her crying in the woods. He seemed to want to make her feel better by telling her how miserable he was. But being trusted by him had made her feel a bit better, and she'd found herself telling him about her brother, and how he'd died of asthma when he was only three years old. She'd trained herself to talk about Hugh without crying, but she didn't say anything about her father who'd had a breakdown afterwards and took too much of his own medicine. And she didn't tell him about Gelyn. Although she very much wanted to.

She almost thought she could trust him. Almost.

Today, one way or another, she was going to go back to the wood alone to call Gelyn out of his tree and make sure she was not imagining it. But she had to do it without Aunt Tiny or Eddie knowing. It was Eddie who would give the game away by scouting around the farm looking for her. That would alert Aunt Tiny that she had gone off alone. While Gwen collected the eggs she concocted a plan and avoided her overly cheerful aunt for the rest of the morning.

Gwen had dinner with Aunt Tiny at twelve o'clock, and then, slightly earlier than usual, she went down to the stream. In her cardigan pocket was a folded bit of paper and a drawing pin. She'd also brought a bottle of water for an offering, and the pocket knife that her father had given her, much against her mother's wishes. It was small but had a very sharp blade as well as a bottle and tin opener. It would be safe at the bottom of her deep skirt pocket.

Once she was past the sightline of the studio, Gwen ran down the hill to the stream as fast as she could. She placed the folded note on the railing of the bridge and fixed it with the shiny drawing pin. The next part was more difficult. She'd only ever gone to Quarry wood by the road from Netherwood's drive, but this time she would need to find her way round the wood to the south and then come through fields onto the road further up the hill. That way Aunt Tiny would assume she was still at the stream with Eddie.

Gwen began by following the stream uphill. There was no path, and it was rough going. She tripped, dropped the water bottle and grazed her knee on a rock, but she didn't stop to wash off the blood. She had to be quick. If Eddie saw or heard her, he would want to come too. Luckily the water bottle had not broken.

When Gwen estimated she had reached the edge of Netherwood land, she turned left up a steep slope of young trees and decaying fallen leaves. By the time she'd reached the top, she was panting for breath and her hands were covered in the green mould that rubbed off the branches. On her right, there was a field sloping up the hill. Gwen climbed over the fence. A herd of sheep eyed her from a distance and bleated insistently. If she kept to the field edge and squeezed through the hedge, she wouldn't draw attention from the farm buildings and then she could rejoin the road.

But that was easier said than done. The hedge was mainly hawthorn and wild rose. Going through it would have torn her clothes to ribbons. Gwen walked up until she came to the wooden gate. Hill Top farmhouse, with all its many windows, was clearly visible from there, so anyone who happened to be looking out would see her trespassing and perhaps tell her aunt. But the only alternative was going back. She looked both ways, swiftly climbed the gate and jumped into the road.

As she walked past the farm entrance she heard raised voices in the yard near the large brick barn.

"That's my final offer, not a penny more!" a loud male voice was saying angrily. "You should take it now, or the price will go down and down for that useless bit of land. Who else would want to buy it?"

Gwen ran on until she reached the path into the wood and hid behind a tree while she got her breath.

A car door banged shut, and an engine spluttered in the farmyard. She put her head round the tree to watch the road. The car was large and gleaming black – the same Vauxhall Twelve that she and Eddie had seen a couple of days before. It was driven by a red-faced man with a big hat. His expression was unpleasantly smug.

Gwen came out from her hiding place. That horrible man had to be Mr Morrison of the quarry. He was pressuring the farmer to sell the wood, if that was the 'useless bit of land' he mentioned. What if the owners of Hill Top did decide to sell? She had to speak to Eddie to find out what they could do to stop it happening.

But first she needed to talk to Gelyn.

She ran through the wood all the way to the gully, then stopped and listened. There was no sound from the farm or the valley, just the distant cawing of the ravens, and nearer, the clear notes of a robin. She scanned the trees for it, but could see nothing through the leaves.

She knelt down by the holly tree and poured out the water around its roots.

"Gelyn," she said in a whisper, her hand on the smooth pale bark.

He appeared suddenly, as if coming out of mist. Gwen sat back hard on her heels and nearly fell over backwards.

"Oh!"

He was grinning and smacking what should have been his lips.

"You again!" he cackled. "Why have you fallen over when it was you that called me?"

The sound of his laughter was like twigs snapping underfoot.

"You came very quickly, I was just surprised," she said, staring at his little face which looked even stranger when happy. He quickly changed to a grumpy look.

"And? What do you want?"

"Umm. I just wanted to …" she began, kneeling down again and leaning towards him. "I brought you some water," she finished.

"And some blood," the little creature observed, cocking its head.

"What?"

"You are bleeding, Gwendoline, and some of your blood is in the soil around my tree. So now you can ask me these things you want to know."

"What do you mean?" she said.

"You are very uninformed. I thought a girl of your name would know more of the laws of the forest," Gelyn said dismissively and moved towards the tree, his arm branch outstretched.

"No! Don't go again! I *do* want to ask you something," Gwen said, reaching out without thinking and touching Gelyn's shoulder.

"Ow!"

Her finger had felt a prick, like a sting or the sharpest of thorns.

"I am not to be touched," the tree spirit said angrily. "I am sacred Holly, strong and sharp, and I'm not a pet." He rustled his prickly leaves and stepped away from her. "I can spare only a few moments before I go."

"I'm sorry," Gwen said, her sore hand at her mouth. "I didn't mean to!"

"No, you are very ignorant and unused to our ways, I can see that. The man who came before you was different. He is much missed."

"What did you mean when you said a girl of my name should know more? What's special about my name?"

"*Gwen-dolen* is your name, in the old tongue," he said with deliberate emphasis. "It means 'bright, fair bow'. And it was the name of one of the queens long ago, the wife of the wise magician, Merlin." Gelyn looked thoughtful. But then his expression changed to one of spite. "And this name brings sadness to the elves, because bows are made of yew wood, and that is why there are so few yew trees and realms for the elves left. They were cut down for the making of the strong British longbow!" the creature cried. "They didn't make them of holly!" he chortled.

"That's not nice," Gwen said. "If men cut down the elf homes to make weapons, no wonder they don't like people."

"Now you are on their side? You are a curious one, Gwendoline," Gelyn said, staring at her crossly.

"I am on your side," she said quickly. "I came to see you because you are so ancient and wise."

Gelyn settled a little.

"May I ask you another question?"

"If it doesn't take too long."

"Will I be able to see the other tree spirits? Ash and Oak and the rest?"

Gelyn looked a bit put out.

"Yes, if you know how."

Gwen waited, her expression bright and interested, but he didn't elaborate.

"Do I need to give them water and blood too?"

"Don't ever give blood to Oak. He will take great offence!"

"Why?"

"You don't understand anything!" Gelyn wailed.

"Please tell me," Gwen asked, putting on her most pleading expression.

Gelyn sighed.

"The trees have signs – follow the signs. Holly and Hawthorn have red berries or haws; therefore we will appear for the offering of blood. I have sharp prickles, and Hawthorn has thorns, we appear for the offering of tears as well. Ash and Beech are tall and strong like fountains; they only accept the purest water from a spring."

He glared at Gwen, checking that she was listening carefully.

"And Oak is the hardest, but if you have seen the tree's wood and its galls, you won't be surprised that he will only appear for whisky and ink."

Gwen was not sure what 'galls' were, but there were so many things to find out.

"What about Elder?"

"You don't want to bring out Elder, I told you before! He works for the elves."

"I'm sorry, I forgot," Gwen said quickly. "Gelyn, why does the birdsong sound different to me? I can't understand it, but it sounds like words I almost know."

The little creature got to his feet and pointed into a tree behind her head. A robin came flying out of it and landed on his hand. The bird stood there, watching Gwen warily with its dark glassy eye, its thin legs gripping the twig finger, swaying very slightly.

"Can I touch it?"

"No! People always want to touch. Just watch and listen."

The robin began singing, and again it felt like a half-remembered song, something she'd heard when she was a very small child. She almost understood its meaning, and then the idea dissolved.

"The man who came before you, the one you call Anders, was only just beginning to understand this after listening for many years. Perhaps you will hear it clearly one day. But you must be silent and listen with all your mind."

A raven flew over the gully and landed on a nearby ash tree frightening the robin, which streaked away towards the tangle of an ivy-laden tree. Gelyn shook his head and began moving towards his holly.

"May I ask you one more thing, kind Gelyn?"

"The listeners have arrived," the tree spirit observed, cocking his head towards the large black shape. "Speak quietly, unless you want the elf lords to know your business."

She looked over at the raven, which was preening its feathers.

"There is another above us," Gelyn said, pointing upwards.

A very large bird was on the branch of a spreading beech tree behind Gelyn's holly. It stared at her.

Gwen licked her dry lips. She leant forward and cupped her hands around her mouth.

"What can protect me against the Greencoats?"

"Oh ho!" Gelyn shouted. The raven above them flapped its wings in surprise and upset. "You are not as ignorant as I thought!" He swayed as if a wind was blowing in his branches. "Now away with you, listeners!" He crackled his leaves loudly, and his tree did the same until the threatening sound was too much for the ravens, and they pushed off their branches and flew away to the north.

"The elf lords and ladies do not like that name. They find it demeaning and disrespectful." Gelyn smiled wickedly. "They say their coats are not poor green leaves like ours, but elfish silver that reflects the light of the forest. But Greencoats they are in this part of the country, and Greencoats they will remain!" he shouted.

Gwen flinched.

"Won't they be angry?"

"They can't hurt me," he said proudly. "And they are far too haughty. So you want to know how to protect yourself? Are you sure you don't fancy a spell in their domain?"

Gwen shook her head, shivering at the thought.

"They treat you well, and there are beauties and treasures beyond imagining," he said clicking his twig fingers.

Gwen's mind was suddenly filled with a vision of a tall room, full of light, and beautiful with carved wood and silver ornament. Tables were set with golden plates and cups, and an enchanting melody was playing. The food steaming on the plates smelt delicious. Gwen's stomach rumbled.

She shook her head violently and stared crossly at Gelyn.

"Did you do that to me?" she demanded.

Gelyn's smile was not entirely pleasant. He shrugged his narrow shoulders.

"You should know what pleasures they have to offer you. Very well. I wouldn't want them to have all the amusement." And the tree spirit bent so close to her she feared another shock if he touched her.

"This is what you must keep on your person in the wood to protect you from their power" he whispered in her ear.

Chapter 13

"What do you mean we need to stop him?" Eddie asked, staring at Gwen as if she'd gone mad.

"I told you, Mr Morrison is trying to buy Quarry Wood. If he does, he will knock down all the trees. We have to stop him," Gwen said, looking up at him from where she was squatting on the bank of the stream.

Eddie scratched his head.

"How do you know?"

Gwen looked down at her bare feet in the stream.

"Just overheard them arguing."

"And this all happened yesterday, when you said in your note that you were preparing for school and writing letters to your parents?" Eddie asked accusingly. He threw a stick at the water.

Gwen kept her burning face turned away.

"Yes, I just walked out to get some fresh air."

"You are such a bad liar," Eddie said scornfully. "Most girls are."

"That's a stupid thing to say!"

Eddie let out a long breath and leant against the slim trunk of an ash.

"So you went up to the wood yesterday by yourself."

"Yes," Gwen admitted, head still down.

"You know, if you don't want me around that's fine. I'll leave you alone. But I think it's pretty mean to lie to me and leave me out, while you go off to the place that I showed you." He pushed himself away from the tree and started walking in the direction of his farm.

"No! Eddie, it's not like that. I like doing things with you. Please don't go!"

He stopped walking but didn't turn around.

"You'd better tell me what is going on, or I'll just let you get on with it by yourself." His voice was tight with hurt.

Gwen climbed up from the stream and sat down on the bridge.

"I'm really sorry. I promise I'll tell you everything. I just had to go on my own to check that I wasn't going mad."

Eddie came back and sat a little distance away from her. He wouldn't meet her eye.

"It's something about the Greencoats, isn't it?" he asked.

It took a long time to explain everything, and there were several points when Eddie looked sceptical, but he didn't laugh at her.

Gwen waited for what seemed a long time before he said anything.

"Will I be able to see him, do you think?"

Relief ran through her like a drink of cool water.

"You believe me!" Gwen said.

"Like I said, you are a terrible liar. I'd know if you were making it up."

"Thanks," Gwen said, hiding her smile.

"So, do you think I'd be able to see the spirit – what's his name, Gelyn?"

"I don't know. But my aunt said I could go up to the wood if I was with you, so why don't we go now, and we can ask him?"

"You can do it. He sounds like a grumpy old man. You have to give him offerings of blood? That's very creepy."

"Hardly any." Gwen looked down at the graze on her knee, which was no more than an ordinary scab now. "It was just a scratch."

"Still," Eddie said uncomfortably.

"Well, do you want to go or not?" Gwen said, suddenly full of energy. It would be wonderful if they both could see Gelyn, and then she could share the problem of the wood and how to save it. And she wouldn't feel so alone.

"Yes, but isn't it a bit late to start today? It must be getting close to five o'clock." Eddie looked doubtfully towards the meadow where the tree shadows were lengthening.

"We have two hours at least. Come on, it won't take long." Gwen got to her feet and started pulling on her shoes.

"All right, but my mother will be angry if I'm late for tea. Where's your crazy dog, by the way?" Eddie said, looking around.

"He's probably still hiding from the cat in Aunt Tiny's studio."

"Poor lad," Eddie said with feeling. "How embarrassing."

They stopped at the house for water and headed up the road, neither of them saying much until they were past Netherwood boundary.

"Who owns Hill Top Farm?" Gwen asked.

Eddie frowned.

"The Whitchins," he said. "Lived there for generations. They own all those fields." He swept his arm up and down the left side of the road.

"What about the wood?"

"Yes, I think they own it," he said uneasily. "But there has always been a footpath along it, so we are within our rights to walk there." He picked a piece of long grass from the verge and put it in his mouth. "What did the man look like who was arguing with them?"

"I couldn't see him very well, but he wasn't tall. He had a big hat like a fedora, and he was driving that new black car we saw."

"Could have been him," Eddie mused.

"Do you think they would sell him the wood?"

"Nope. It would make a mess of their fields if they quarried away the ridge. They'd have to be really desperate."

The entrance to the farm was coming up on the left.

"We don't get on with the Whitchins," Eddie muttered. "Had a disagreement at market about stock, and my dad and Mr Whitchin haven't spoken for about six years."

Gwen stared at him, wide-eyed.

"Just because of some farm animals?"

"He tried to swindle us! He was going to sell my dad poorly ewes when he knew they had sheep pox. Charged us over the odds as well."

"Blimey. I believe you," Gwen said, dropping back a pace.

"It would have contaminated our whole flock."

"Sorry I asked," Gwen whispered.

They walked on in silence until they reached the path.

"So how are we going to do this?" Eddie asked, chewing the stalk of the grass and then spitting it into the undergrowth.

"I'll summon Gelyn and then ask him about you. I think that would be best."

"If I give him some of my blood, would that make me see him?"

They were walking single file so Gwen couldn't see his face.

"I don't think it works like that," she said carefully. "I think the only reason I see him is because I saw the elf first."

"So that's what they are – the Greencoats? Their official name, I mean."

"I think so," Gwen said, suppressing the desire to giggle. It was strange to suddenly be the expert in such matters.

"What did it look like? The elf you saw?"

"I could only see its arm," Gwen admitted. "It was sort of shining and gave off this wave of coldness." She shivered involuntarily, deciding not to tell Eddie about the fingers that had been reaching down towards her.

"So you haven't been up there since? To the yew tree?"

"I went back, but there wasn't anything there."

"I suppose you can't make them appear if they don't want to," Eddie said, sounding disappointed.

"Gelyn told me I was lucky that Boo and I got away." Gwen shook her head. "I think it would be better to steer well clear of them."

"But he's told you what you need to get to protect yourself now, right? So if I got the same, maybe I could see them without being in danger?"

"Yes, he told me, but I'm not sure how it works." Gwen said, her hand going automatically to her pocket. The rowan berries had been easy to find. But the red thread had been difficult. Eventually she had pulled a bit of ruby wool out of the end of one of Aunt Tiny's Persian carpets.

They had reached the entrance to the gully and stopped, looking up towards the holly tree. Then they both turned to look back down the path at the same moment.

Something was coming up fast behind them, not caring how much noise it made. Eddie pulled Gwen round behind him, but she pushed him aside. She knew that panting sound.

Boo was running towards them, his tongue and fur flying out behind him. Gwen barred the path, putting her arms out to catch him, but he dodged her and ran past, his eyes wild and unseeing, his tail standing straight up.

Gwen picked herself up and started running after him as fast as she could.

"The elves have enchanted him again," she cried. "We have to catch him!"

"I guess he's not that old after all," panted Eddie, just behind her.

Boo was well ahead of them already, crashing through the wood. But Gwen knew where he was heading. As she and Eddie reached the base of the hill below the glade, two ravens rose from the treetops, calling to each other with harsh croaks.

"They know we are coming!" Gwen cried, her heart bursting as they started up the slope. A seeping coldness enfolded her as they scrambled over the last few yards of shattered stone and branches and stopped short at the edge of the ring of elders.

"Don't go through the glade," Gwen whispered. Her body was trembling. She could see a shimmering figure standing in the centre of the trees, arms extended, fingers rigid.

"Look!" Eddie cried. He wasn't pointing at the elf, but at the dark shadow under the old yew. Boo was digging frantically at its roots, soil flying out behind him. Eddie had started to run towards him.

"Wait!" Gwen shouted, lurching after him, hoping the protection of the rowan berries in her pocket would extend to him. She reached out and grabbed his hand.

As they ran towards the yew, tripping and stumbling, Gwen saw a shadow opening in front of Boo, an emptiness, as if the roots had moved to one side and made a hole or a tunnel. Gwen wanted to run faster but her lungs were full of coldness.

A pale hand reached out from the darkness of the hole. It was the same hand, with the same long rigid fingers.

They touched the dog's head.

"No!" Gwen shouted.

Eddie let go of her hand and tried to lunge forward to grab Boo's back legs.

"No!" she shouted again and pulled Eddie back. "They will take you too!"

They stopped short a few paces from where Boo had just been. The hole in the great dark red roots of the old tree was filling itself in with rich black soil, getting smaller and smaller.

"No!" Gwen screamed.

She felt a great fury rise up inside her, and she turned to the glade, her fingers splayed out in front of her, gripping Eddie with her other hand.

She did not know what came out of her mouth. Words of anger, perhaps a curse. She did not consciously understand them.

The reply was laughter, like cracking ice.

A voice spoke inside her head.

"Once we have chosen our quarry, we do not let it go. You should take more care of your loved ones, *Gwendolen*."

And with a sudden snap of wind, the voice and the cold were gone. The two ravens rose from the yew tree into the evening sky.

Eddie was staring at her, wide-eyed and bemused.

"Are you all right?" he asked.

She nodded and let go of his hand.

"You are safe now; they are gone."

He shook his hand as if it hurt.

"You've got a strong grip for a girl," he muttered. He looked around at the yew tree, chewing his lip. "Should we go and get some spades or something?"

"Spades?" Gwen said, wiping away the angry tears that had fallen down her cheeks.

"To dig that crazy dog out. He can't be that far down." Eddie pointed to the small opening where the hole had been.

Gwen gave him an impatient look.

"Didn't you see? The elf lord has taken him," she said. "You can't get him out by digging. He's in their realm, probably eating all his food off golden plates by now," she said angrily and turned away. "The Greencoats have stolen my dog!" she screamed at the glade.

In the distance a raven called, then the forest returned to its creaking silence.

Gwen pressed her fists to her eyes.

"The only thing we can do is summon Gelyn. He will help us get Boo back. He has to!"

Chapter 14

"How did Boo get here anyway?" Eddie said, as they slipped down the hill back to the path. "You'd think he'd have learnt his lesson from last time."

"He must have followed us – or smelt where we went. Maybe he thought we'd take him for a walk, then when he entered the wood, the Greencoats enchanted him," Gwen said, her teeth chattering. She felt utterly exhausted, as if she'd just trudged through a snowstorm.

Eddie didn't look very well either. He was stumbling more than usual, and his face was uncharacteristically pale.

"Was there one of them in the glade? Is that why you were shouting?"

Gwen didn't answer for a while.

"I don't know what I was saying. I don't know what is happening to me." She was glad Eddie was walking in front of her so he couldn't see her face.

"At least neither of us got taken," he said. "We could have been. It happened about seven years ago to a boy my brother knew." He stopped and looked at her. "Hey, what was the thing that Gelyn said would protect you?"

Gwen reached in her pocket. The bunch of rowan berries was wilted and bedraggled. The frayed bit of thread hung in a limp bow around the stems.

Eddie raised his eyebrows.

"Don't look like much, does it?"

She put the bunch back in her pocket.

"Guess I ought to get my own. Save my hand from being crushed in your mighty grip," Eddie muttered, looking around at the trees. He walked on a little way. "There's one." He pointed down towards the edge of the wood where it met the field.

He scrambled down the debris of rock and wood, eventually coming back with a large bunch of bright red berries. Gwen had taken advantage of his absence to blow her nose and wipe her face. The trembling was finally subsiding.

"Does it have to have a silly bow?" Eddie asked, panting a little.

"Rowan berries and red thread," Gwen said. "It doesn't have to be a bow, but it has to be red and tied in a knot."

Eddie rooted around in the pockets of his short trousers and brought out a penknife a bit larger than her own.

"What are you going to do?" Gwen asked uneasily.

"You'll see." He tugged his white and green checked shirt out of his waistband and examined the hem until he found a loose thread, pulled it carefully until he had unravelled about five inches, and cut it off with the knife. He folded the knife again and shoved it in his pocket. Then he rolled up his sleeve and turned his arm over to examine an old scab on his elbow. With his fingernail, he pulled it off and a drop of deep red blood began welling out. Eddie ran the thread through the blood until it was all stained. Then he rolled his sleeve down again and grinned at her.

"That's got to make it even more powerful," he said, tying the damp thread around the stem of the rowan and shoving it all into his pocket. "Seems a bit daft, though."

"Come on, let's go." Gwen started off down the path. "It's getting late. We've got to get Boo back before dark."

"I don't think that's going to happen, Gwen," Eddie was saying behind her, but she ignored him and didn't turn around until they reached the gully. There was the bottle of water just off the path where she had dropped it when Boo ran past. She picked it up, went straight to the holly trunk and splashed the water over the roots and her shoes.

Gwen touched the tree.

"Gelyn. We need you!"

She looked around, but there was no sign of him.

"Gelyn!"

Nothing.

Eddie was looking worried.

"Please, kind Gelyn, we need your help!"

He came then, snapping his twig fingers and looking more cross than ever, gesturing at Eddie.

"This is not right. I'm not a creature in one of your zoos to impress your friends."

Gwen sank down onto her heels.

"Eddie is here to help." She turned to gesture at him, but Eddie was not listening. He was standing oddly still, unseeing, swaying slightly.

"What have you done to him?" she cried.

"He is experiencing the life of a tree for a little while," Gelyn said, with satisfaction. "He cannot be part of our conversation. Now tell me what you want and be quick about it. I am growing tired of you, bothering me every day," and he turned his head half away from Gwen as if in a sulk.

"Please, dear Gelyn, tell me how to rescue my aunt's dog from the Greencoats."

Gelyn looked at her out of the corner of his eyes.

"They are happy now, aren't they," he said with a hint of slyness in his voice. "You should take more care of your loved ones, *Gwendolen,*" he imitated the elfish voice. Then he started his cackling laugh, and Gwen had to press her lips together to stop the cross words coming out of her mouth.

Gelyn eventually stopped laughing and looked up at the sky.

"There are no listeners near, so I will tell you one way to regain your loved one from the halls of the lords and ladies."

He held out his hand.

"You may touch me. It won't hurt."

She put out her fingers tentatively. As soon as she felt the hard wood of his hand, her mind filled with a scene so real that she wanted to step into it, but there was no speech or any other sound.

A woman stood before a tall yew, even older than the one in their wood. She was wearing peasant clothes, but in her hands was a beautiful golden cup, ornate and set with gemstones. Its shape was familiar to Gwen. The poor woman held out the cup to a tall stern elf, who took it and bowed. Then from behind him, a little girl was brought forward, dark-haired, walking as if in a dream. Her mother opened her arms and lifted the girl, kissing her face.

"They like the treasures of the church, the elves do. They like to use the chalice and paten as cups and plates. They eat from them, believing it gives them more power," Gelyn said in her mind. "Bring them the church treasures as a ransom."

"I can't steal from the church!" Gwen answered. The thought of it made her feel a bit sick.

"That is the easiest way to get your loved one back," Gelyn said in a persuasive tone. "Are you sure you won't do it? The church will simply get another cup and plate. They are only made of metal after all, but your dog is a living thing."

Gwen imagined entering the church after the service and slipping the chalice inside her choir robe.

But then, out of the corner of her eye, she saw Rosie Brown, pointing and shouting as she tried to run out of church.

"No. I can't do it. Tell me the other ways."

Another scene filled her mind. This time an old man stood at the base of a different yew tree. He knelt down in front of it. A hole, like the one Boo had entered, opened amongst the roots, and he was pulled in. When he had completely disappeared, a wild eyed, long-haired boy climbed out and looked around as if just awakened.

"They will often accept an exchange. Not always. It must, of course, be an equal exchange," Gelyn said in her mind.

"Do you mean someone would have to take Boo's place?"

"Yes. If the elves accepted the replacement."

Gwen opened her eyes. She took her hand away from Gelyn and stared at him.

"But whoever goes in would be trapped in the elf realm."

"That is what an exchange means," Gelyn shrugged.

"Isn't there any other way?"

"No other schemes have succeeded."

Gwen tried to imagine what was happening to Boo now. Was he frantically running around, barking and trying to find a way out?

"Will they hurt him?"

"They don't hurt in that way. They will care for him and keep him alive. The prisoners of the elves are not aware of time passing. They are not distressed. But this you must understand," Gelyn said severely. "The elves love nothing better than watching men and women in confusion. It gives them great pleasure and entertainment. And the elves are always hungry for diversion."

"That's horrible," Gwen cried.

"It is no worse than what men do to all other animals," Gelyn said, his eyes bright and hard. "And to each other." He stood up and spread his branching arms out wide. "It is late, and I am tired."

With a cracking of sharp leaves he disappeared.

Eddie lurched forward like a felled tree and just managed to stop himself from crashing on top of Gwen.

"What?" he croaked, leaning against the holly. "What happened? Did I fall asleep?"

Gwen got up. It was sunset, and pink clouds were gathered on the western horizon.

"Gelyn turned you into a tree temporarily," she said bitterly. "Come on. It will be dark soon. We should go."

"But what happened?" he said, stumbling after her.

"I'll tell you when we are out of this crazy wood."

Chapter 15

Aunt Tiny was standing in the kitchen doorway when Gwen and Eddie came down the drive. The moon was almost full, rising beyond the house as a pale shadow in the twilight.

"There you are!" she said. "Have you got that dog with you?" She was peering out into the dark yard.

"No," Gwen said, "we haven't seen him. I thought he was with you in the studio." She turned to look at Eddie who was standing awkwardly behind her. "Bye. See you tomorrow," she said to him and walked past her aunt into the kitchen.

"Oh, I thought Boo went off with you. He was desperate to get out of the studio, and he headed off in the direction you had gone." Aunt Tiny stuck her head out of the door again. "Eddie!" she called. "If you see Boo on the way home, could you bring him back, please?"

"Yes, I will," Eddie promised in the distance.

"Gwen –" Aunt Tiny began.

"I'm sorry we were late back, Auntie. I must just spend a penny," and Gwen raced through the larder to the loo.

When she came back again, having washed her face and hands and composed her expression, Aunt Tiny was putting on a headscarf and a light jacket.

"I'll just go and call him before it is completely dark. He doesn't usually stay out so late. Gwen, can you stir the pan and make sure it doesn't burn?" She pointed to the cooker.

"Shall I come with you?" It was awful seeing the worry on her aunt's face.

"No, no. Just stay here and mind the supper. I don't want to lose anyone else!" She shut the kitchen door behind her.

Gwen stood at the cooker, slowly stirring the onions, mushrooms, bacon and leeks, her mind racing. It would be impossible to tell Aunt Tiny what had actually happened, but not telling her was torture. There was no way of getting Boo back until tomorrow, if at all.

She would just have to accept that it was going to be a very difficult night.

Gwen sniffed and held her breath. When she was trying not to cry, this usually worked. Perhaps she could blame tears on the onions, but it was important she didn't look upset in front of her aunt. She put the kettle on to make a cup of tea. Tea always helped.

It seemed a long time before the door opened and Aunt Tiny came in.

"No sign of him," she sighed. "I went down to the stream and then up and down the road calling. I wonder if there is a bitch on heat at one of the farms. That might be why he was so desperate to get out. But it's never happened before."

She untied the scarf from under her throat and came over to the cooker.

"Is that a cup of tea? Lovely. Just what I need."

Aunt Tiny poured the tea into two mugs and looked in the milk jug.

"We are nearly out of milk, so tomorrow morning we will go up to Hill Top Farm and get some. We can ask if they have seen Boo. I know they have a female collie. He might well be hanging around there."

She passed Gwen a cup.

"You are very quiet, young lady. Has anything happened?"

"No, I'm just hungry. And worried about Boo," Gwen said, wondering if she looked as guilty as she felt.

"You mustn't worry about him." Aunt Tiny reached for the kettle. "He can look after himself. He'll be back tomorrow, scruffier than ever. What were you up to in the woods?"

The sudden question caught Gwen by surprise. She pulled out a chair and sat at the table, cradling her cup in her hands.

"We were at the stream most of the time, then we went looking for fossils and exploring."

"I'm so glad you and Eddie get on," Aunt Tiny said, pouring some hot water in the pan with the vegetables and throwing in some salt. "I was worried you would be bored here. There aren't as many children about as you have at home. But you and Eddie have the same interests, I guess. What a piece of luck!"

She turned to the kitchen door, her head cocked.

"I think I heard something outside. Gwen, can you go and see if it's Boo trying to get in through the gate, please?"

Gwen pushed the chair on the flagstones and got up. She left the door open and walked out into the yard. The night was clear and the moon shone brightly. Over the wood, a constellation was rising that could be The Plough. Her father had pointed it out when she'd been very small, lying side by side on a lawn in a park, long ago.

"Boo!" she called. It was awful having to pretend and knowing he couldn't possibly come home without some terrible exchange with the greedy elves. As if their entertainment was worth all this heartache and worry.

A shape ran out of the darkness towards her, and her heart skipped a beat. But it was only Cleopatra, swaying as she ran. She'd been stalking mice by the chicken run, no doubt. The cat started rubbing herself against Gwen's legs.

Gwen bent down. Cleopatra's eyes were glowing in the reflected light from the kitchen window. She scratched her behind the ears.

"You are a big bully," she whispered. The cat meowed hungrily and wove in between her legs.

"I would rather have Boo than you any day," Gwen said, stroking her back. The cat sat down at her feet and began to lick one of her front paws.

Gwen stared at her, paralyzed by a thought. She bent down and tried to pick Cleopatra up, but the cat ran off towards the kitchen, as if she knew what Gwen was thinking.

She followed her back into the light.

"It was just the cat," she said to Aunt Tiny, who was cutting a loaf of bread.

"Oh, that's a shame," Aunt Tiny said, distractedly. "Here, can you butter these while I add some cream to the soup?"

They ate their supper unusually quickly and in silence.

Aunt Tiny collected the bowls.

"Gwen, I'm going to go out to see if I can find him one more time before bed. It would be lovely to have him back. We will both sleep more easily. So I'm sorry, no piano tonight. Will you be all right here on your own for a bit?"

Gwen nodded solemnly.

"Good girl. Take yourself off to bed if you're tired." Aunt Tiny already had her scarf on and was slipping her feet into her boots. "I have a feeling he may have gone down the road. I didn't try Seven Springs Farm. They also have dogs," she said, halfway out of the door.

Gwen waited until she heard the click of the gate in the yard. She got up and went into the larder. Cleopatra was licking the last of the oil out of her dish of sardines. She was a large cat and would be heavy to carry. Gwen would have to put her in the basket that she'd come in, and that might not be easy to do given how hard it had been for Aunt Tiny to catch her in the first place.

Where was that basket now?

Gwen looked round the larder. The walls were covered with shelves crowded with jars of pickled onions, chutney, jam and other, more mysterious, things. Finally she spotted it hanging on a hook above the larder door.

She left the basket where it was. The plan had to be worked out properly. She mustn't rush it. Gwen went back into the kitchen, put away the supper things and then climbed up the stairs to where Anders' painting hung.

She stared at it for a long time as the plan took shape in her mind. The more she looked at the painting, the more she noticed amongst the branches shapes she hadn't seen before, like the outlines or shadows of hands and the profiles of elegant heads, cleverly worked into the very trees themselves. He *had* known the elves, or at least enough to paint their likeness. Gwen traced one of the shapes with her finger, and Gelyn's admonition about the robin sounded in her head.

No. People always want to touch. Just watch and listen.

Perhaps there was something she could learn from the birds that would properly help her, unlike Gelyn who seemed so cross all the time. He *had* told her how to get Boo back, but it was hard to know if he was really on her side, or if it was all some elaborate game for him.

Maybe he liked confusing people and found it amusing. In the painting, his face was rather sly, while Anders' friend, Ash, had a calm and open expression.

Perhaps she should try to summon her. Maybe not all the spirits were as grumpy as Gelyn. Maybe Ash would be glad to help.

To summon that spirit, she would need to know her name. Her proper ancient name.

Gwen ran up the stairs. She had a good idea of where to look for that information, but as she reached her landing, she heard a distant thudding that was growing louder.

The planes were coming, and Aunt Tiny was outside in the dark under them.

Gwen ran back down the stairs to the kitchen and opened the door.

They were not flying over the house but coming from the west where the River Severn flowed, probably following the reflection of the moon on the water. There were seven white and red lights drumming the night air.

Just a few moments later, as the last plane was disappearing over the hill, Aunt Tiny came through the gate. She was breathing heavily.

"Nothing. Not that Boo could hear my calls over that racket," she said angrily, waving her hand in the direction the German planes had gone. Her face was shiny with sweat. "He'll be hiding under a hedge somewhere." She looked around the kitchen as she took off her jacket. "Is the cat in?"

Gwen nodded.

"Good. I'll shut her in the larder and leave the kitchen door ajar in case Boo decides to come home in the night. Now, would you like to sleep in my bed, or on your own?"

"I'd like to do some reading please. I'll be fine in my own bed, Auntie."

"That's the spirit, Gwen. We can get used to anything, can't we?" Aunt Tiny said, giving her an awkward pat on the shoulder.

It took Gwen a long time to find the right place in the book. She had to wade through pages of bizarre beliefs about various spirits such as pixies and banshees. The plants that had special properties were more interesting. She paused over the description of fern seed she had dismissed before. Could it possibly be true that it made one invisible? If so, it would be highly useful. Then she came to the list of ancient British tree names from the Celtic languages. There was Gelyn for Holly, Derwen for Oak, and for Ash – Onnen.

It had been pure water that Ash accepted as an offering – pure water from a spring. So that was the next thing to find.

She shut the book. The following day was Friday. School began on Monday. If she was going to get Boo back, she needed to act quickly and without Aunt Tiny or Eddie noticing.

As they'd walked down the road, she'd told Eddie about the two ways of getting creatures back from the elves. He'd whistled and said a rude word. It was not fair to involve him. He would just be endangered if he tried to help. The elves might think she was going to swap him for Boo.

No. She would do it on her own.

Chapter 16

The next morning, Aunt Tiny and Gwen took it in turns to push the old wheelbarrow up the hill. It was very heavy and the wheel seemed unsteady. It kept juddering and veering off course. Finally they reached the farm entrance and stopped to get their breath. The day was already hot. Flies buzzed around them, trying to land on their faces.

"Over here," said Aunt Tiny, picking up the handles of the barrow and pushing it towards the other side of the farmyard.

"Mrs Whitchin?" she called. "We've come for some milk!"

A middle-aged woman, her hair scraped back in a bun on the back of her head, emerged from a low dark building.

"Mrs Høeg," she said, and turned to stare at Gwen. "Who's this?"

"My niece Gwen. She's come to stay for a while from Birmingham. She drinks a lot of your milk," Aunt Tiny smiled, "so we've come to top up."

Mrs Whitchin didn't smile in return.

"Heard what happened last night?" she asked, hands on her hips. She spoke out of the corner of her mouth, as if one side of it didn't work. "Bombs in Bridgnorth. destroyed the Squirrels Public House. Two deaths, far as I know. That's them planes coming back from the towns, dropping their filthy loads on us." She pointed at the sky and looked at Gwen accusingly.

"Oh goodness. How awful," Aunt Tiny said. "Your sister wasn't hurt, was she?"

"No. How much milk are you wanting?" the woman asked, moving off.

"One full can please, and I just wondered if you've seen my dog, the brown scruffy one? He disappeared yesterday, and I thought he might be bothering your collie?"

They followed the woman to the dairy where eight large milk cans and a butter churn stood in the cool stone room.

"Not seen him since yesterday evening. Heading up the road, he was," she said. Each word had to work hard to make it out of the small opening in her mouth.

"Oh. You saw him yesterday? What time was that?" Aunt Tiny asked eagerly.

"After milking." Mrs Whitchin picked up one of the full cans as if it were light as a feather and carried it out to the yard. "Where's your cart?"

"We brought the barrow today. Had to give up the pony, she ate so much!" Aunt Tiny said with false brightness.

The woman jerked her head upwards.

"Bloody Nazis," she said. "Be nothing left when they've finished with us. Invasion coming within weeks, they say."

Aunt Tiny's mouth twitched. She pointed at the barrow.

"Gwen and I will manage it fine."

Mrs Whitchin accepted the coins with the smallest of nods and disappeared back into the cowshed.

Between them, Gwen and her aunt lifted the can into the barrow.

"You'll have to hold it steady while I push," Aunt Tiny said.

They set off awkwardly.

As the hill got steeper, it became even more difficult to stop the milk from tipping out of the can.

"Gwen," Aunt Tiny said as the road levelled out just before their gate, "are you sure you didn't see Boo yesterday evening? If he went past the farm, he was probably following you into the wood."

Gwen kept her eyes on the can of milk.

"No, I'm sorry Aunt Tiny. I didn't see him. I wish he were back right now. I miss him so much."

"I do too, darling." She watched Gwen open the gate, her expression thoughtful. "But now I'm wondering – if he didn't find you in the woods, what did he find?"

Later that morning, Aunt Tiny went looking in the woods on her own. Gwen was sewing the tear in her skirt that she'd forgotten to repair all those days before. Sewing always made her feel calmer, and she hoped it would help her think through her plan. From her bedroom window, Gwen watched her aunt turning right out of the gate with a lead in one hand.

What would Aunt Tiny feel in the wood? Would she notice the strangeness? It was horrible to think of the elves laughing cruelly as she walked along, calling and calling. Gwen tied a knot in the thread and snapped it off between her teeth. Her sewing was not nearly as neat as her mother's, but it would have to do.

A movement by the gate drew her eye. Someone was coming down the drive, a girl with bobbed brown hair and a yellow skirt – Rosie, from the choir. She cast a critical eye over the house and walked towards the kitchen door. Gwen went quickly down the stairs. Rosie stood in the kitchen doorway, looking around.

"Hello," Gwen said, standing by a chair.

"Hello, my father said I should come and see you because you are new, and he said you should be told what to expect. Can I come in?" Rosie walked into the kitchen and sat down in Aunt Tiny's chair.

"Yes," Gwen said, "of course." She sat down too and then got up again. "Would you like some water – or tea?"

"Water. It's very hot. I've never been down here before. Only as far as the Whitchins. Is all this your aunt's?" she asked, turning round and looking out of the kitchen window.

"Yes. She's out at the moment." Gwen put a glass of water in front of Rosie and sat down carefully. "It's nice of you to come."

"It wasn't my idea," Rosie said, frowning. "My father is always trying to make me do exercise. He thinks I sit around and read too much." She pushed her hair out of her eyes. "So he makes me go out every day."

"Oh," Gwen said. "What do you read?"

"Cowboy stories mainly," Rosie said. "Anyway, why don't we go to your room, and I'll tell you all about school and who the troublesome children are. That way at least you will be less ignorant, my father says."

Gwen led Rosie up the stairs with a heavy heart. There was no knowing how long she would stay, prattling on. And if she didn't leave, Gwen would not be able to go to the wood herself. She pushed open her bedroom door and Rosie went in and straight to the window.

"Are those your chickens?" She did not wait for a reply. "You can see a long way. Do you see the planes flying over? I heard that they dropped lots of bombs on Bridgnorth last night. My aunt knows one of the women who died. Have any of your family died in the air raids?"

She turned round to look at Gwen, who quickly shook her head.

"Lucky you," Rosie said. "My mother died when I was born."

Gwen opened her mouth to tell her about Hugh, but shut it again. It would sound like she was boasting that her brother had died.

Rosie glanced around the room.

"That's a big book." She went over to the bed and picked up *Traditions, Superstitions, & Folklore.* "Have you read this whole thing?"

"Not all of it."

Rosie flipped through some of the pages, while Gwen's fingers itched to take it away from her.

"Oh, my grandad used to do this. Dowsing. He was well known for it. Farmers used to ask him to locate the water on their land with his dowsing rod. He would find it every time," she said proudly. "My father won't even try it though; he says it's unchristian."

"Do you mean your grandfather found springs of water?" Gwen asked, a kick of excitement in her chest. "What's a dowsing rod?"

"It's a forked stick, that's all," Rosie said importantly. "The magic is in the hands of the dowser. Apparently it runs in families, so I should be able to do it. When the stick is over fresh water, it jumps about in the dowser's hands, no matter how far down the water is. It also works for buried metals. They used to get dowsers to find good places to dig mines. It should say how to make a dowsing rod in here."

Rosie sat down on the floor with her back to the bed and the book on her lap, and Gwen sat down next to her.

She ran her finger down the page full of dense, old-fashioned lettering.

"Yes, here. It says *Divining rods*, that's the same as dowsing rods," she interjected, "*must be made of hazel or rowan.*"

"Again the rowan," Gwen said to herself.

"What?"

"Nothing. Does it say anything else about what to do with the stick?"

Rosie scanned the page.

"No, but my dad told me that his dad had a favourite tree he used to take them from, and always at twilight. I think it was also important if the moon was waxing or waning, but I can't remember which."

"Well, we could just try it anyway and see if it works without cutting it at a special time," Gwen suggested, trying not to let her excitement show.

Rosie looked at her seriously.

"You're not going to make fun of me if it doesn't work, are you? And then tell the others at school that I'm strange. That would be mean."

"Of course not. I promise!" Gwen got up and reached deep in her pocket. "I know where there's a rowan tree. And we can see if there's a spring in the field somewhere over there. Look, I've got a pocket knife to cut the branch with."

Rosie got to her feet and looked at it critically.

"I suppose that will do, although I bet it's supposed to be made of cursed iron or something."

They spent a long time below the rowan tree at the edge of Aunt Tiny's property, discussing the virtues of each forking branch above them. In the end it was Gwen who had to climb up to get the chosen branch, as Rosie was not allowed to climb trees.

Gwen had to sit on one of the branches and saw away at the stick at arm's length. Eventually it dropped to the ground, and she slithered down the tree trunk, grazing the skin on her hands and legs.

Rosie was holding the stick in one hand.

"Here, give me the knife a minute." She trimmed off the leaves and the berries. Gwen picked up the latter and pocketed them, her previous ones having become soft and limp.

"That should do," Rosie said, holding the smooth bare stick in both hands by the forked ends. "I think you are supposed to hold it very loosely on the palms of your hands so the energy can make it move about." She started walking down the field.

Gwen watched her for a moment, then got up to follow. It all seemed so ordinary. She found it hard to believe that anything special was going to happen.

"Let's go and try the field over there," she called, pointing to the meadow where the pony used to graze.

Rosie stopped walking and looked back.

"I don't think there's anything here. But maybe I'm meant to be doing it with my eyes shut or something."

In the end, Rosie got very hot and tired from going up and down the field in the blazing sun, and, to give her credit, she did not pretend to have felt anything.

"You probably have to cut the rod at the right time for it to work. Or you don't have any springs on your farm," she said grumpily as they trudged back towards the house.

"We could try somewhere else another time," Gwen said. She'd picked up the dowsing rod when Rosie threw it on the ground in disgust. The forked end was sticking out of her pocket.

"Maybe," Rosie said, unenthusiastically. "I think I'd rather read my book though. I'm going home for my dinner. See you Sunday."

Gwen stood in the yard, watching her go up the drive.

"What on earth were you two doing?" a voice said behind her. Eddie's amused face peered out from behind the hen house. "I thought you'd lost your wits even more than before. And with Rosie-busybody-Brown too!"

Gwen walked over to him.

"She's not so bad. We were using a dowsing rod." She held it out for him to see. "It's meant to tell you where springs and treasure are. Maybe you can make it work?"

"No chance. I can't even see the elves. Obviously you should try it. I couldn't understand why she was doing all the walking around with her eyes closed. But aren't you meant to be finding your dog, not water or treasure?"

Gwen put a finger to her lips. She wasn't sure if Aunt Tiny had come back from the wood or not.

"You are not allowed to make fun of her about it at school, Eddie."

"What, she's your best friend now?" he asked huffily. "You haven't told her about the elves and Boo have you?"

"Of course not!" Gwen said. "You are the only one who knows. I just think she's a bit lonely. She's only got her father, after all."

"And he's no barrel of laughs," Eddie said, with feeling. "I promise I won't make fun of her. My lips are sealed." He twisted an imaginary key between his lips and threw it over his shoulder. "Hey, I've thought of a plan," he said. "After dinner, I'll tell you down at the stream."

Chapter 17

Gwen let Eddie talk about his plan for a long time. He had a wooden cup and plate that one of his brothers had made on a pole lathe when he was training in woodwork. Eddie would paint them to look like a communion chalice and plate from the church.

He would do it this evening, and then they would go up to the wood tomorrow when he'd finished his jobs on the farm. They would take the fake treasures to the yew and trick the elves into exchanging them for Boo.

Eddie was very pleased with his scheme and was keen to get started immediately by finding the gold paint that Anders had kept in his studio to gild the picture frames. He was sure it was still there.

Gwen followed him back to the house to look for the paint. Aunt Tiny was working. They could hear the faint sound of music from the wireless as they went through the yard. Gwen tried to look as excited as Eddie when he found the old box of gold powder in one of the drawers. He checked the amount in the box, and stuffed it into his pocket.

"I think you have to mix it with oil," he said, nearly running out of the Anders' studio. "I've got some brushes. Tomorrow I'll get up extra early so we can go before dinner." Eddie was already out of the kitchen door, when he stopped, took several steps back and stood on the threshold. "Hey, Gwen. You're going to do this with me, aren't you? You do think it will work?"

"It might work," she said carefully. "It's worth a try."

"Yeah, that's what I thought," he said, reassured. "See you tomorrow."

But by tomorrow Gwen's own plan would have started, and it was important that Eddie knew nothing about it. It was already after three o'clock, and she had so much to do before her aunt came in from her studio for tea.

Gwen went round the back of the house and up to the gate, out of view of her aunt's studio. If there was anywhere that would have plenty of springs of fresh water, it was Seven Springs Farm down the road, where her aunt had gone last night. She would take the dowsing rod and hope that she wouldn't have to do any digging, as walking along with a bottle and a spade would be hard to explain. Gwen wiped her damp hands on her skirt and set off. She felt a bit breathless. It was too frightening to think about what she was doing, so she started singing one of the silly music hall tunes that she'd practised with Aunt Tiny.

It turned out to be quite a short walk to the Seven Springs sign and the farm lane. As she'd thought, the Quarry Wood ridge began just behind the farm. These were the distant farm buildings she had seen all those days before. If she walked up the farm lane, there should be a way into the wood.

The farm dogs barked loudly as Gwen walked past the barns. One brown and white collie came rushing out on a chain, its mouth a lather of red tongue and white teeth. Another black and white collie was loose and ran after her, but soon stopped barking and sniffed her hands and legs thoroughly before turning back.

No one else came out. It was harvest time. They would all be making hay and piling straw into big bales in the middle of fields to stop enemy planes from landing during the expected invasion.

But to Gwen, the war seemed distant. Even the planes going overhead didn't feel real anymore. It was the fight to get Boo back from the elves and their strange magical world that was taking all her attention.

One field width separated the farm from the wood. At the corner of it, below a large beech tree, there was a wooden gate. The path through the trees stretched up the hill behind it. Gwen climbed up and sat on the top rail. From there she had a good view across the farmland. A tractor was going along the furthest field, followed by two figures turning over the straw with rakes. It looked like very hot work.

Gwen's hands were unsteady, but she took the dowsing rod and held it experimentally. It seemed completely inanimate. It was a ridiculous plan, really. What did she think she, just a ten-year-old girl, could do against all the elf lords and ladies? She should go home and forget about Boo. It was hopeless.

She let the stick drop out of her hands and fall onto the dry ground.

A song of clear liquid notes, like golden bells and pure flowing water, came from the branch above her. A robin. The plump bird hopped onto a lower branch almost within Gwen's reach and opened its tiny yellow mouth.

Gwen listened and listened, watching the bright, black eye of the bird as it sang and the way its orange breast feathers ruffled in the breeze. Very slowly, she began to see a picture in her mind – a path with a trickle of water flowing next to it.

When the robin finally flew away, Gwen jumped down from the gate, picked up the dowsing rod and went out on the farm lane again. There was the water running in a muddy trickle down the side of it. Why hadn't she noticed it before? She followed the water uphill, until the lane stopped at a gate into a field of sheep.

In the end she managed to find the spring, a patch of bright green, spongy grass in the middle of the field. It was a messy business, and the ewes were very curious. She had to kneel right in it to half-fill her bottle. The water looked a bit muddy, and there were some blades of grass mixed in it, but, if she let it settle, hopefully it would be pure enough.

She walked back to the gate and climbed over.

It felt very different entering the wood knowing that the elves would be watching her, and probably laughing at her. She began to sing again just to keep her mind off it. The robin appeared on a branch ahead of her, keeping pace as she went up the path looking for the beautiful ash tree from the painting. It filled the pauses between verses with its own music.

She found the tree in a part of the lower wood that she'd not been to before. The ash was tall and broad, and its drooping branches hung down low enough to touch. The robin landed on one of its limbs.

But Gwen stopped, frozen in front of it. She couldn't remember the ancient name of Ash. It had completely disappeared from her mind. She had gone to all the trouble of getting the spring water for nothing. She sat down on the ground, crossed her legs, and screwed her eyes shut. Perhaps the elves were confusing her. What had she forgotten?

Her hand went to her pocket. There were the rowan berries, but there was nothing around their stems. She hadn't tied them. That was why she was confused, and why she'd felt so hopeless when she'd been sitting on the gate before. The red thread had been thrown out with the old berries. She would have to use Eddie's trick, and thinking about that made her wish she'd brought him along.

A thread was easy to pull out of her white sock, but the blood was another matter. The graze on her knee was all healed over. She gave the fresh pink skin a scratch and thought hard. When she'd been poorly last winter, a nurse had taken blood from her fingertip with a pin.

Gwen went to the hedge, found a thorn, and pricked her index finger, squeezing it until a drop of blood bloomed from the tiny hole. She ran the thread through it until it was scarlet, tied it around the stem of the berries and put them in her pocket.

The name came back almost instantly.

"Onnen," she whispered. She pulled the stopper out of the bottle, poured the clearest water out of the top of it onto the ground between the ash's most prominent roots and touched the trunk.

"Onnen, please come and talk to me."

Onnen arrived more slowly than Gelyn had. She was slender and rounded, and her hands had long smooth fingers of the slightest twigs. Her face was neither happy nor sad but seemed to constantly change, like the light that touched the ash leaves on her soft dress.

"Who has woken me?" she asked. Her voice was whispery, the sound of a soft wind across a stand of trees. She did not seem cross, or even curious.

"My name is Gwendoline," Gwen said, kneeling down. "Please will you help me, as you helped my friend Anders?"

The tree spirit looked at her more intently.

"You are very young." She came towards Gwen and touched her. There was no shock, but a feeling of lethargy made Gwen's eyes droop a little. "You know the spirit Gelyn, who is always awake. He has spoken to you. And yet you are sad." The tree spirit took her hand away. "You did not know my friend Anders," she concluded, stepping back and beginning to fade.

"Please don't go, beautiful Onnen. Anders' wife is my aunt," Gwen said hurriedly. "I didn't know him in person, but I live in his house and I need help to get the dog he sent back from the elves."

Onnen tipped her elegant head to one side.

"What you have told me is hard to understand," she said softly. "Gelyn is more alert than I. Soon I will begin to lose my leaves and settle for the winter." She ran her hands down the layers of her leafy dress. "I used to speak with Anders all through the spring and summer, but hardly in the autumn, and I never come out in the winter." She shivered and her form rustled and danced with light. "You may ask me a question, child. I speak only briefly. I speak only truth. Then I will sleep again."

Onnen yawned, covering her small mouth with her hand.

Gwen took a deep breath.

"Please tell me how I can enter the elves' realm without them seeing me."

When Gwen got back to Netherwood after collecting the things she needed, it was almost twilight. She hoped Aunt Tiny wouldn't have left her studio already. If she saw that Gwen had disobeyed her about going alone to the wood, she might be alert to the other things Gwen was going to do.

But as luck had it, Aunt Tiny came through the kitchen door just as Gwen was washing her hands.

"You didn't see Boo when you were out, I suppose," she said in a resigned way, taking off her apron. "I am now wondering if he's gone up to the main road and been injured." She pulled off her headscarf and ran her hands through her hair. "Or of course, he could have returned to wherever he came from in the first place." Aunt Tiny's face seemed more lined than usual, and there was a nasty rash on her neck.

"Maybe that was all the time I'm allowed with Boo. Maybe he's gone to help someone else who needs cheering up." She was trying to smile, but Gwen could see that her aunt was close to tears. She turned back to the sink.

"No, we looked all along the road and in the woods, but we couldn't find him anywhere. Should we go and ask in Much Wenlock tomorrow?" Gwen suggested.

"Yes, maybe," her aunt said, the kettle in one hand. Aunt Tiny was looking her up and down and chewing her lip. "Gwen, you are looking very much muddier and grubbier than you ever have before. I can't imagine what your mother would say. It is certainly time for you to have a bath, and I'll wash out those clothes so they can dry on the cooker for tomorrow."

But that would mean Gwen would have to wear her smart clothes to go to the wood in the night. And all the special things that were stashed in her pockets would need to be taken out.

"Could we please wash tomorrow, Auntie? I'm so tired, I really want to go to bed early."

"Do you? Are you feeling ill?" Aunt Tiny looked at her and a line formed down the middle of her forehead. Gwen wondered if Aunt Tiny had ever seen Hugh when he was very sick. She recognized that concerned expression.

"No, I'm just tired," Gwen said. "I played with Rosie all morning, and Eddie and I walked miles looking for Boo."

"Then school will start before you know it." Aunt Tiny filled the kettle. "Yes, I suppose we can wash tomorrow, although I will insist on wiping those knees before you get into bed. They will make the sheets filthy!"

Chapter 18

Cleopatra's greed turned out to be an advantage. After midnight when Gwen entered the larder, fetched the basket down by the light of a single candle, opened the last tin of sardines and wedged it in the bottom of the basket, the cat immediately jumped inside, and Gwen was able to put down the flaps and secure it through the loops with the stick without any fuss at all.

It had been hard to wait until after the planes had gone and returned. Hard to wait even longer so that Aunt Tiny was definitely asleep before Gwen crept down the stairs into the cold kitchen, the door still propped hopefully open in case Boo found his way home. But she wasn't tired. Her senses were so alert to every sound that she felt more awake, more alive, than ever before.

Gwen had worried that Cleopatra would be upset about being trapped in the basket and make noise that would wake Aunt Tiny. But the cat was busy gobbling the sardines, and, by the time she finished them, Gwen had already walked up the drive and was opening the gate.

The moon was full and it was a clear night. She could see the road and even the individual spears of grass on the verge. If Eddie had been with her, he would have started chewing one of those. Gwen pushed that thought firmly away.

The disadvantage of the greediness of the cat soon became obvious. Gwen had to put the basket down every few minutes and swap hands. It would take a long time to climb the hill, lugging her enormous weight, but this was the only way. Eddie's plan was bound to fail. If he had ever seen a real elf, he would have realized that they could not be fooled by painted wood. It was an insult to their cold, hard intelligence.

Gwen didn't want to exchange Cleo for Boo, but if she had to, at least the cat would have plenty to eat in the elf halls. Food was, after all, what Cleo loved most of all, and Aunt Tiny needed her dog back. She was miserable without him.

Gwen passed the entrance to Hill Top Farm with great care. The last thing she needed was a dog to start barking. Behind her an owl called from Netherwood Coppice, and the answer came from Quarry Wood. Perhaps they were speaking about her, noticing where she was going. Gelyn had never mentioned owls, but maybe the elves did have nighttime sentinels who took over when the ravens went to sleep.

She had hoped to arrive in the wood unnoticed, but, as she stepped onto the dark path, she knew that would be impossible. There were all kinds of creatures awake in the woods at night, and one of them was sure to raise the alarm.

Gwen stopped and put the basket down for a moment. It rocked sideways as Cleopatra moved around, trying to find a comfortable position. Then the noises of the forest began to reassert themselves: the small rustlings of voles and shrews, the wind in the branches, the distant sound of a fox calling.

Gwen touched the dowsing rod in her pocket to make sure it had not fallen out. The back door to the elves' realm was well hidden, Onnen had told her, but the rowan divining rod would point it out as a way to their gold and silver treasure. And Gwen thought she knew a good place to start. She picked up the basket again and continued down the moon-mottled path.

She couldn't quite remember the location of the tree with the hole through its base she'd seen on her very first time in the wood, so she went very slowly. When she came near, she found a flat bit of ground and propped the basket upright, so the cat wouldn't tip it over. It was a good spot, easy to find again. If her first plan did not work, she would come back for Cleo and attempt an exchange. In the meantime, with all that food in her, the cat should have a nice long nap.

Gwen took the dowsing rod out of her pocket, held it in her open palms and turned slowly on the spot. As she got three quarters of the way round, the rod jumped in her palm like a nervous mouse.

She stopped and took a step forward. There was a soft crack as she stepped on a hidden branch. She lifted her other foot and lowered it slowly. The rod jerked down. She was not heading towards the tree with the hole. The rod was taking her down the slope towards the field behind Hill Top Farm.

"Not to water," she whispered. "Please, I don't want a spring now."

She went forward step by step, the shadows of the tree branches making it hard to see where she was being led. After twenty paces, at the very edge of the field, she saw an old tree that marked the end of the farm boundary. It was a large oak, its base surrounded by spurs of new growth so it looked bearded and wizened. She took another step towards it, and the rod dipped suddenly, as if it would jump out of her hand. She stopped, her heart thudding so loudly in her chest that she couldn't hear anything else.

In the dark it was a frightening tree. Its low shoots looked like long fingers, and the shadow it cast in the moonlight was of an outspread hand. Gwen took another step towards it, and the rod jumped again as if it were filled with an electric charge.

There was no doubt.

She put the rod in her pocket and touched the rowan berries. Her body wanted to run away, but her mind at least was clear. From her other pocket she removed the small bit of folded paper in which she had collected the seeds of the fern that grew by Netherwood stream.

Onnen had said that they would allow her to enter the realm of the elves without their awareness.

Fern seed did not make a person invisible to other people, but it did hide a human from the eyes of the otherworld. Gwen would have to swallow them, or they would have no effect. And that was an unpleasant business.

Gwen tipped them all in her mouth at once to get it over with, like Hugh used to take his hated medicine. The urge to cough them all up came instantly, but she swallowed hard three times with her hand over her mouth and then wiped her streaming eyes.

She was doing things her father would be horrified by: taking untested medicine, being in the woods alone at night, entering a hostile realm. But she thought he would have liked the clear sky full of stars, and perhaps the excitement of an adventure.

Gwen took the dowsing rod in her hands again and went forward. It led her round to the other side of the tree, where, amongst the whips of young wood at its base, there was a gap, perhaps large enough for a rabbit but not a ten-year-old girl.

Gwen knelt down, holding the bunch of rowan berries in one hand and the dowsing rod in the other. She reached into the hole and tapped the berries three times on the hidden ground. She pulled back and stared at the hole, gripping the berries hard between her fingers. Nothing seemed to happen at first, but gradually she realized that either she'd grown smaller or the hole much bigger, because it was now as wide as her shoulders.

Gwen looked around. It was unwise to go into any creature's den at night down a narrow tunnel, but there was no one there to insist that she shouldn't – no one to save her from having to enter the awful, dark hole, only the distant moon overhead and the glimpse of stars beyond the leaves.

She pushed the rowan berries to the bottom of her pocket and held the dowsing rod in front of her like a toy sword. Then Gwen crouched down and entered the darkness on her hands and knees.

Loose soil fell on her head when she brushed against the roof of the tunnel. It trickled down her neck, making it itch. There was not a speck of light. Below her, there was both soil and stone. She knew her knees were already bleeding.

The smell of damp earth and rotting leaves was very strong, like her father's vegetable bed when he'd turn it over with his garden fork. She crawled a few more paces, and the tunnel began to slope downwards gradually.

Gwen put one hand out. The sides of the passage were definitely further away. She reached up. There was more room above her head. She crawled a bit faster and quickly felt a change in pressure in her ears. She put both her hands out beside and above her but could feel nothing. She had entered a chamber, or a cave perhaps. She cautiously stood up, feeling giddy, straining her eyes for any light. The pricking on her hands made her feel nauseous with fear. What if all the elves were sitting in this room able to see her, while she was blind?

"My daddy wouldn't buy me a bow wow," she sang in a whisper to the emptiness.

No reply. All she could hear was the scrape of her breath on her sore, dry throat and the thudding in her chest.

Gwen put her shaking hands out in front of her and shuffled slowly, diagonally to the left, until her fingertips touched a wall. She stopped and felt the surface of it. It was curving wider, making the opening bigger. Gwen stood with her back to the wall and took the dowsing rod in both her hands, slowly sweeping it across what she imagined was the scope of the room. It jerked excitedly in the direction of the widening wall.

Keeping her foot dragging along the base of the wall, she followed the tugging of the rod blindly for many steps until her foot came to an emptiness. She felt for the edge, the cold stone where the wall continued in a new direction. So this was another tunnel, and the dowsing rod wanted her to go down it.

It was a much taller passage, but very narrow and cut steeply downwards into the earth. Gwen forced her feet to move forward, keeping one hand on the wall, the other gripping the dowsing rod straight out in front of her. The tunnel seemed to go on forever, just darkness and muffled air – full of the sound of her footsteps and loud breathing.

Then as if her eyes could not stand any more emptiness and had to create something for her mind to see, a distant glow of green light appeared ahead, like a will-o'-the-wisp. She couldn't tell if it was near or far, large or small. It hung in the darkness, and she had to force herself not to run towards it.

Gwen stopped and steadied herself against the wall of the passage. She rubbed her eyes and looked down towards the green light. It seemed to be an opening into a room, still quite a long way off. She shoved the rod in her pocket and touched the rowan.

The pricking on her hands was very strong. She must keep her head. It wanted to turn around. Her whole body wanted to run back, up the tunnel, through the cave and out into the open air and then all the way back to her bedroom.

But Onnen had instructed her very clearly. The rowan's magic only allowed travel in one direction in the underground realm. She must face forward. If she turned all the way round to look behind her at any point, even just instinctively for a moment, or if she took a step backwards, the protection of the rowan would stop. She had to keep moving forward and facing forward. No backward steps, no backward glances, otherwise she would come under the power of the elves.

A faint sound of voices rose from where the green light glowed.

Gwen took a deep breath and told her shaking legs to start moving down the tunnel towards it.

Chapter 19

The hall was not the one that she'd been shown in the vision by Gelyn, but the long tables covered with gold and silver plates were similar. Here the feast was over, and the plates were mainly empty. Small groups of elves sat in conversation, their voices chiming like streams of water flowing over stone.

There were two other entrances coming into the hall, wide and well lit compared to Gwen's tunnel. A few elves were leaving down these corridors, but the hall was still crowded – still full of their strange, elongated faces and bodies. Seeing so many together made Gwen sweat with fear. They almost looked human. Almost beautiful. But they had the cold paleness of those who live underground, and those who don't know love.

She stayed the shadow of the tunnel, watching. The sensation of pricking on her hands was so strong that it felt like many needles stabbing her at once. The green light was coming from a large central opening in the ceiling of the oval hall and cast a vital illumination over everything: the swirling wooden columns carved with vines and leaves, the long shining tables, the faces of the Greencoats.

It was hard to look at the elves and hard to stop looking. Their skin shimmered like light on satin. Sometimes they were only faintly there, sometimes fully physical. It reminded Gwen of the way rainbows look close and distant at the same time. And there was something about their beauty and their indifference, the shape and colour of their eyes, the regal way they held themselves, both male and female, that made Gwen feel as if she were a small mouse cornered in a room full of snakes.

She tore her gaze away from them and crouched down so that she had a better view of the floor. If Boo was in the room, he would be sniffing along looking for scraps under the tables. He wasn't under the nearest one, but she couldn't check the others from her position. There was no way to avoid it; she would have to go further in, and the sooner the better. She did not know how long the fern seed would last.

Gwen stood up. Gripping the rowan in her pocket and holding her breath, she inched from the darkness of the tunnel, glancing left and right out of the corners of her eyes. The elves might not be able to see her, but they would certainly feel something if they bumped into her.

She kept to the wall, her face forward, shrinking against it as two elves got up from the nearest table and walked past her towards one of the bright passages on the other side of the hall. They showed no sign of noticing her, continuing their conversation and looking straight through her. The elves walked with a peculiar motion, their shining gowns and capes swirling with clouds of silver.

Gwen watched them glide away. Breathlessly, she took a few more steps. When she was about a quarter of the way round the curving wall, she could look down the length of the long central table. It was still occupied by many elves, drinking from silver goblets. Their voices were melodious, liquid, and unintelligible. Gwen blocked it out. If she became absorbed in the music of their voices, she might forget why she was here and become trapped.

She crouched down and squinted under the table. In amongst the chair legs and the elf gowns, there was something moving. A creature that was neither slim nor elegant, but hairy and scruffy. Its nose was leading it along the floor systematically, not an inch unexplored. Gwen estimated that Boo was about twenty yards away and gradually moving in her direction.

This part of her plan was sketchy at best. She had not dared think of actually being in the realm of the elves, or how she would get hold of her dog whilst completely surrounded by them. Now that she saw Boo, she had to resist the urge to run down the gap between the tables straight to him. If she did that, all would be lost. She must stay still and quiet, face forward and wait.

One of the elf ladies on the other side of the hall stood up and began to play a stringed instrument with a long neck, like a stretched mandolin. The notes were as pure and clear as the spray from a waterfall.

Gwen shook her head. Again there was the danger of losing herself in the strange beauty of it. Boo was just a few yards away, and she must concentrate.

She took the piece of bacon she'd saved from breakfast out of the pocket where she'd stowed the dowsing rod. Boo would still be enchanted, but that did not mean he had forgotten such a delicious smell. Surely nothing could make a dog indifferent to bacon.

The elves at the table had turned towards the musician, and all other noise had stopped. She broke off a piece of the bacon and held it out, wafting it up and down so the smell would travel to the dog's nose.

It took a few moments for Boo to look up from the floor. Perhaps all he saw was the smell of bacon floating in the air, but he ran under the table to her, mouth open, tongue out. She brought the bacon close to her and let him eat it, while she grabbed his collar with her other hand.

Boo looked up at her, an expression of sudden bewilderment in his eyes. Then he opened his mouth and let out a happy and excited bark. Gwen froze. She heard the sound of chairs being moved. The music had stopped.

She kept hold of Boo's collar and tried to hide most of her body behind the dog. A male elf in a long flowing cloak was standing at the end of the central table. He pointed at Boo and spoke loudly, as if commanding him. But Boo was not listening. He was nudging Gwen's hand for more bacon and barking happily. The elf's eyes narrowed. He pointed again, and the command left his mouth like a blast of cold wind.

Gwen let go of Boo's collar and took her hands away so she wouldn't be touching any part of him. The effect was instant. Boo's expression changed, becoming unseeing and trancelike again. He went straight to the elf and sat down in front of him. Without contact with the rowan through Gwen, Boo would do exactly as the elves instructed him.

She crept forward a few paces along the wall while Boo was being admonished. Then the elf in the long cloak straightened up and spoke to the room. Presumably it was an instruction for the music to continue. He evidently had authority over them, as all the elves sat down immediately and turned towards the musician.

But the elf in the long cloak did not. He walked over to the place where Gwen had been crouching and began to examine the floor. It was stone, so her feet shouldn't have left a print. The elf bent over and touched the floor with the tip of his long finger. Perhaps dirt from the tunnel had come in on her shoes. He scanned the sweep of the wall. Gwen ducked her head, unable to stand the thought of his lizard eyes on hers. When she eventually looked up again he was sitting back at the table, facing the musician like the other elves.

But Boo had disappeared.

She looked as far round as she could without turning her head, but he was not under any of the nearby tables. Gwen felt tears starting in her eyes. She had held him, had felt his warm breath on her face, and now he was gone. Again.

She was going to have to leave without him, after coming all this way. She would go back to sad Aunt Tiny, who needed Boo so much, who still believed that Anders had sent him to be with her. And what's more, to stay facing forward, Gwen would have to go around the whole room, making the full circuit of it before she would be hidden again in the dark tunnel.

She gripped the rowan in her sweaty palm and squeezed her eyes shut, wishing she wasn't alone. Wishing for Eddie, or Aunt Tiny, or her father to appear and to know what to do.

Gwen opened her eyes again. The music played on in the hall, notes and iridescence glinting off its cold, stone walls.

Gwen took a shallow breath and carefully, quietly took a small step.

She had gone twenty miserable paces or thereabouts, when something warm and hairy nosed at her pocket. She only just stopped herself from shouting his name and turning round to hug his furry neck.

Instead she bit her lip and got the remains of the bacon out of her pocket, holding it tight in her hand. This time she would not touch him. He became too excited when he recognized her. She kept her eyes forward and put the hand with the bacon behind her. Boo started licking the little bit of bacon sticking out. She took a step forward, and he moved too. If they kept going, they would eventually reach the sanctuary of the tunnel. But it was a long way. The hall seemed to be getting wider and colder all the time.

Boo was licking and nibbling the bacon, and after each step she allowed him a little bit more of a taste. Half-way round the room, they had to go directly behind the musician and in front of the eyes of all the elves. Gwen crouched down and hoped that they couldn't see her with all the tables and chairs in the way, even if the fern seed's protection had worn off.

The bacon ran out when the entrance to the tunnel was only a few yards away. She could not touch, or call or tempt Boo any more, so she ran for it, unable to look back to see if any elves had noticed that their precious captured dog was leaving. Gwen went five paces into the tunnel and then put her hand behind her as far as she could. A tongue tried to lick the gaps between her fingers. Boo was still there. She put her other hand out to feel the side of the passage and started climbing up the slope into total blackness, praying that the dog would follow the promise of bacon all the way.

She counted forty steps in the dark before she stopped. It was far enough away from the elves to risk touching the dog. If he barked they wouldn't hear him.

"Boo!" she whispered.

A cold wet nose pushed her hand. She tried to reach back for his collar, but it only met empty space.

"Come on boy," she said, waving her arm frantically behind her. There was the sound of panting, but was it getting more faint? Perhaps he was running back down to the elves' hall to sniff out better tidbits on the floor.

"Boo!" she called.

There was nothing there.

"There's no dog better than Boo," she sang huskily, waving her slimy hand behind her. "Everyone knows it's true."

A wet thing began licking her hand enthusiastically.

"Oh good boy, Boo," she said, and, as slowly as she could, she brought that hand forward, while reaching back with her other one, feeling the brush of fur on her wrist. She ran her hand down the back of his head, took hold of the collar and pulled.

"Come on boy – let's go!" she cried.

He jumped up, barking and licking her face.

"Good boy," she said, "now we have to run!"

Boo was more than happy to oblige. He dragged her for thirty lung-burning paces up the slope, but she managed to stop him as they came out into the first chamber, the sound of his panting and hers echoing off the domed walls of the cave.

Keeping hold of his collar with one hand, she felt around for the dowsing rod to help her find the way to the first tunnel. But there was nothing in that pocket, and in the other one, just the bunch of rowan berries. The rod must have fallen out as they'd run up the slope. Now it was somewhere back in the dark tunnel, and they were standing in pitch blackness with no way to find it. Turning back would mean certain capture: Gwen lost to her family for years, and Cleo trapped and hungry in the basket in the wood.

Gwen put her hand in her mouth to stop herself from crying and knelt down next to Boo. She just had to remember very clearly which way she had come. It seemed like hours ago. She hit her head lightly with her fist.

"Think!" she hissed at herself.

She had come out of the tunnel, and the dowsing rod had taken her along the left wall. She had kept left, all the way until she had been led down the steep passage. So now it would be the reverse. She had to go right, her right hand along the wall until she came to the first passage. Was that correct, or was the elf magic confusing her again? She jerked her head. It throbbed with exhaustion.

Gwen rubbed her thumb along the dent in her finger made by years of holding a pencil too tightly, her only reliable method of telling left from right. With a trembling finger tracing the right-hand wall, and Boo panting and pulling on her other hand, she headed into the cave. It seemed a very long time before she felt the shock of emptiness as the wall disappeared under her fingers. Was this the correct passage? It seemed much further than it had been the first time. She must have missed the way out. If she went into the wrong tunnel she could be lost forever in the enchanted labyrinth. Either that or she'd be found by the elves and come under their power.

Gwen stood touching the edge of the passage and taking shallow, ragged breaths. There was a slight movement of air coming out of the opening – and a familiar smell. Her father's vegetable beds. Earth.

It must be the way out. It was going up, out of the stone and into the soil. After the soil, there would be starlight. She tugged on Boo's collar, and they went up into the next darkness together.

Chapter 20

It became harder and harder to keep hold of Boo as the passage narrowed around them. When they came to the last bit where she had to crawl, Boo was in front and she was holding on to his tail. He didn't like it.

And strangely, it was getting quite light, as if there was more than just the moon outside. Gwen spat some soil out of her mouth and clung on to the end of Boo's tail as the light became blinding. She crawled forward, her eyes screwed up tightly against the pain of the sudden brightness. Boo whined and tried to pull his tail out of her hand.

She opened her eyes a crack. The sun was properly up. She must have been down in the elves' realm for much longer than she'd thought. Gwen pushed herself up with one hand, still gripping the dog's tail.

"Boo," she called. He turned around, showing the whites of his eyes, wanting to run away from the pain in his tail, but he curled round and licked her hand instead. She grabbed his collar. "Sit, boy, sit," she croaked. Her throat felt full of dust.

He sat in front of her, his mouth slightly open, his pink tongue hanging out.

"Good boy, stay with me. I have to hold on to you until we get out of this crazy wood."

She would have a lot of explaining to do when she got back to Aunt Tiny's house. Her aunt would certainly be up by now, and may have noticed that the cat wasn't in the larder. And then there was Gwen's appearance. Her knees were raw and bleeding, her hands too. And her clothes were so stained and dusty, it was hard to tell their original colour.

She must get the cat and go back to Netherwood, then she could explain everything.

Keeping a firm grip on Boo's collar, she scrambled up the slope to where she had wedged the basket, praying that the cat had not hurt herself trying to get out. But the basket was not there, and there was no sign of Cleo.

Gwen stared at the empty space where she was sure she had put it. She turned all the way around. Things look different in the dark. Maybe it was another tree. Boo was sniffing the ground where the basket should have been. She pulled on his collar.

"Come on, we have to find her," Gwen said, tugging him towards the path.

She had a terrible sinking feeling that the elves had found the cat in the night, and, as she was escaping with Boo, they were bringing Cleopatra down through their dark corridors. But Gwen was not going back in there to rescue her. Just the thought of it made her feel icy cold.

She stumbled after Boo as he lunged along the track. They were nearly at the gully, and Gwen knew she hadn't left the cat as far down the path as this. She pulled to a stop and nearly let go of Boo as the back of her hand began to prick painfully.

Gwen looked up.

She was staring into the face of the elf from the hall as he appeared out of an elder tree growing in front of the gully. The cape that had been silver in the hall was green with reflected leaves. His eyes were very pale blue, pierced with a tiny pupil.

"*Gwendoline.*" He stepped onto the path and reached out his long fingers towards her.

She grabbed instinctively at the rowan in her pocket and clung on to Boo, who started barking and lunging forward frantically.

"Get away from him," she shouted. "Don't touch my dog!"

"He is not your dog," the elf said, and his voice was neither loud nor soft but seemed to enter her mind without the need for hearing. She stared at him, the fury of terror rising.

"He's not your dog either," she shouted. "And you can't have him back. I'm taking him home."

The elf looked at her rather sardonically.

"You are unexpected," he said. "We have not been raided for many years. And the one who has done it is a half-grown girl, all alone, against the whole court of the elves." As he said this, another elf, even taller than the first, climbed out of the elder tree and stood barring the path.

Gwen looked around wildly. About five yards away was a young holly tree growing out of the rocky slope. She ran for it, dragging Boo with her.

"I'm not alone!" She reached the tree and threw her arm around it. "Gelyn help me!"

The tree spirit appeared in a crackling of air.

"They can't have him, can they? Tell them!" Gwen cried. "They can't take things away from people just for their amusement. It's horrible! Don't you know what it's like to love someone and lose them? It makes your insides ache. It makes you feel lost and hopeless. It makes you feel like dying! Is that what you want to do to us?" Gwen shouted, hugging Boo around the neck.

The elves stood impassively, staring at her tear-stained, grubby face.

Gelyn went forward and stood between her and the elves, his arms spread out like a branching bough. He seemed taller than before.

"Hear the words of the new friend of the forest," he said in his raspy voice. "She has beaten you at your own game. Her size is no reflection of her courage. Go back to your realm. Instead of pursuing her, spend your time preparing to save your home from the machines that any day now will cut down your tree and dig through its roots."

The elf with the long cape sneered, but the other put a hand on his shoulder.

"Gelyn speaks well. We should not waste our time on noisy animals," he said, looking at the frantic dog, "but on protecting our realm."

"But if we can't protect our territory from a small, dirty girl," the caped elf snapped, "how will we defeat the men with their saws and axes? She should be taken prisoner so she cannot spread information on how to defeat us to other men." He glanced in the direction of the quarry.

"But I don't want you to be defeated," Gwen said, crossly. "I want to save your wood. I would never tell those men how to do anything bad to you or any of your trees." She got to her feet, still holding Boo's collar with her aching arm. "But if you steal the things we love, you make people very angry."

Gelyn pointed at the elves with one hand and at Gwen with the other, his small black eyes gleaming.

"You have the same desire. You both love this wood. You shouldn't be enemies."

Gwen glared at the caped elf.

"They have to stop trying to steal my dog. Otherwise how can we be friends?"

Gelyn turned to her.

"Make a pact."

The elves looked at one another uncomfortably.

"What kind of pact?" Gwen asked.

"You swear to help protect the elves and their realm, and they swear to protect you and not to steal from you," the tree spirit explained.

Gwen looked at Gelyn. She was sure he was getting bigger even as he spoke, looking more regal and less rustic.

"They also have to protect my friends and my family – anyone I bring to the wood," Gwen said, thinking fast.

"And you must promise never to enter our realm without our consent," the taller elf said. The caped elf turned his angry face away, saying nothing.

"Gladly," Gwen agreed. It would be a relief never to have to go down there again.

"Now you must perform the ritual," Gelyn said. Even his voice was changing, becoming less scratchy and more sonorous. "Put your hands out."

The more reasonable elf came forward. He gave Gwen an expectant look, but she kept holding on to Boo.

"How do I know *he* won't take Boo if I let him go now?" she asked, pointing at the caped elf.

The other elf turned his head and spoke words she didn't understand.

The caped elf replied angrily, but he kept his head slightly bent, and did not meet the taller elf's eyes. There were several moments of silence, and then, without looking at her, the caped elf went to the elder tree and disappeared.

The remaining elf cocked his head at her. She noticed that he wore a silver circlet around his brow.

"Is the Queen of the Wood satisfied now?" he said with a hint of mockery.

"Stay, Boo." Gwen let go of the collar and straightened up.

"What is your name?" she asked.

"You may call me Lord Elisael, but unlike these spirits, I do not always come when summoned." His face was impassive, but his tone was proud.

Gwen held out her hand and he took it in his pale grip.

The elf's skin was cool and smooth. As soon as she touched it all the anxiety and fear left her. It felt as though she no longer had any responsibilities or worries. Her mind was blank, and she could just look at the elf's beauty without fear.

She repeated the promises that Gelyn pronounced without thought. Then the elf leaned down, bent his head and kissed her hand. It felt like the sweetness of honey spreading through her arm, removing all her pain.

"You must do the same," Gelyn said.

She bent her head, feeling extremely foolish, and kissed Lord Elisael's hand. Her lips tingled, and, when she looked up, she was smiling without being able to help it.

They both let go.

"It is done," Gelyn said, and he seemed to shrink until he looked like the creature she had first seen only a week before. Boo was sitting quite still, barely breathing, presumably in the tree-state that Eddie had experienced.

Then Gwen remembered.

"Where's my cat?" she said suddenly, waking up from the peaceful trance. "I left her here in a basket, and she's disappeared."

"I cannot help you with that," Gelyn said, and with a snap of his fingers he was gone.

She looked towards the elf lord, but he was dissolving into the elder tree, leaving only a patch of shimmering air.

"Wait!" she called. "Bring back my cat!"

Boo shook himself all over and barked. Gwen grabbed his collar just as he started running.

"Oh no you don't," she said. "We are going home, no more gallivanting. I'm going to lock you in the house, and then I'll come back and find that cat –"

"Hey!" A shout came from behind her. "Hey!" Eddie was running down the path towards her. "Gwen, my God, you're here! And that crazy dog. I knew that was his bark!"

Eddie was pale and grubby, but not as much as Gwen. He pulled up short in front of her, hesitated and then patted her shoulder.

"I thought you were gone for good!"

Gwen felt her cheeks burning.

"But I've only been gone the night. Isn't it still morning?" She glanced at the sky. It looked about eight a.m. to her. "Did Aunt Tiny wake up in the night and notice I was gone?"

"No, you idiot," Eddie said, taking Boo's collar from her and giving the dog a scratch behind the ears. "She noticed you were gone early on Saturday morning. It's Sunday today, and you can't go disappearing into the woods for more than a day without people noticing!"

"What? I went into the elves' realm on Friday night. It can't be Sunday!" Gwen cried.

"Well it is." Eddie pointed in the direction of the town. "The church bells will start ringing any minute."

Gwen felt light-headed. She had lost a day somewhere between entering and leaving the elves' hall. Perhaps in their music, perhaps in listening to their voices. Time had slipped away like water through fingers. But she had got out, and now here was Eddie in flesh and blood.

Gwen looked around the scruffy wood with its fallen trees and mossy stumps.

"What happened to Cleopatra? I never meant to give her to them if I could help it."

Eddie grinned.

"As soon as I saw her by the tree, I knew what you were trying to do. Don't worry. She's fine." Eddie was feeling around in his pocket. He took out a length of string and looped it around Boo's collar. "Eating your aunt out of house and home as usual. When we came up here to look for you yesterday morning, that cat was yowling and meowing, so we didn't have any trouble finding her." Eddie straightened up, holding the makeshift lead.

"Aunt Tiny must be furious with me," Gwen said.

Eddie looked at her and pulled the kind of face that told her she was being thick. He started walking out of the wood.

"Your aunt isn't angry, *idiot*. She's terrified," he said, his head half-turned towards her. "She's been sick with worry. The police were going to start searching the quarry for your body today. She went into Wenlock to telephone your mother at the factory."

"But you told her where I was, didn't you?" Gwen said, following him towards the entrance to the wood. "You told her I would be back?"

"How could I know if you would be back or not?" he said. "I've never waited for someone to steal a dog from the Greencoats before. And you didn't tell me what you were planning," he said angrily. "You just let me get on with my little art project."

He was walking very quickly, looking straight ahead.

"I'm sorry! I thought if you were with me they'd try to take you too. And that would have been awful." She ran a few paces to keep up. "I really am sorry."

Eddie didn't say anything for a while. Then she heard him take a deep breath.

"Well, next time, give me a chance," he said quietly. "It's not much fun being left out."

"I will," she said. "There might be lots of other times."

He glanced back at her, his eyes gleaming, a grin beginning to turn up the corners of his mouth.

"I'll tell you later," she said. "It should be safe for us here from now on." Gwen shook the image of the caped elf's cold frown out of her mind. "But what about Aunt Tiny? What did you tell her?"

"I told your aunt everything. All about Gelyn and the elves and how they wanted to steal the dog. She was kind about it, but I could tell that she didn't want to believe me."

"Let's go, then." Gwen started to run. "We've got to show her that Boo and I are fine!"

Chapter 21

They ran down the hill to Netherwood, arms windmilling, legs burning, and came to a breathless stop at the gate. Boo put his paws on it and barked loudly.

As Gwen opened the gate and he rushed through, they saw Aunt Tiny's red, dishevelled head looking out of the kitchen door, and then she was running towards them, Boo bouncing around her, licking her hands.

She reached out for Gwen and hugged her to her chest.

"Lillian!" she shouted, her voice cracking. "Alfred! She's back, she's here!"

Gwen looked up at her aunt and wiped her eyes.

"They are here?"

Aunt Tiny gave her a gentle push towards the kitchen, her other hand rubbing Boo behind his ears.

"Yes, my darling. They just arrived on the early train. Run and find them!"

But she didn't need to. They were coming out of the doorway, looking so familiar and also unfamiliar. Her mother in her travelling suit, her hair falling limply around her face, her father, looking like an old man until he saw Gwen and smiled.

She ran into them blindly, throwing her arms around them, forgetting how dirty she was. They were kneeling down, holding her, stroking her hair.

"Where have you been, where have you been?" her mother chanted, pressing her head against Gwen's.

Her father got his arms under hers and lifted her up. She put her legs around his waist and clung on as she had done as a small girl when she pretended to be a bear cub.

Gwen buried her face in his shoulder. He smelt of coal and tobacco.

"Come into the kitchen," Aunt Tiny said, patting Gwen's head. "Come on, Eddie, you too. I will make us all a cup of tea and you can tell us everything." She put her arm around Gwen's mother and walked her into the house.

"Daddy," Gwen said into his ear.

"Mmmm?"

She could feel his heart beating against hers, feel his tears wet on the back of her neck.

"Do you have to go back to the hospital?"

"No, Gwennie. I've come back now," he whispered, tightening his embrace. "I'm here to stay."

And he carried her into the kitchen.

Boo was already lying under the table, and Eddie was standing awkwardly by the window.

Her father put her down, and she went to sit on her mother's lap.

"I'm sorry," Gwen whispered, looking down at her hands. "I'm sorry I worried you."

Her mother held her around the waist and kissed her cheek.

"Explanations can wait," exclaimed Aunt Tiny. "You come over here and wash your hands and face in the sink while I get the tea. Eddie, can you get the cups and saucers from that shelf? This calls for a celebration!" She wiped her cheeks with the back of her hand.

"Is the cat all right?" Gwen asked, as she got up to go to the sink.

"She is absolutely fine," Aunt Tiny said. She turned to look at Boo under the table. "But I think some changes may be necessary to keep everyone safe and happy. At the moment she is asleep on your bed, Gwen."

"I didn't really want to get rid of her, it was just in case I couldn't get Boo back any other way," she said without thinking, picking up the lump of soap and turning on the tap.

The pain in her hands as she washed them made her gasp. It was as if the sensations in her body had been switched off, and then suddenly came back all at once. Her head was spinning, hands throbbing, knees stinging, and her back and arms aching. She sat down at the table, feeling like laying her head down on it and closing her eyes.

"Put lots of sugar in that tea for her," she heard her mother saying. The cup was stirred and brought over. "Gwen, here darling, drink this." The teacup was held to her lips.

She took a sip of the hot, sweet, milky tea.

"Look at the state of you." Her mother began wiping Gwen's bleeding hands with her handkerchief. "This calls for a pharmacist, I'd say.

Drink it all up," she insisted, holding the cup again so that Gwen wouldn't have to.

"If only I'd brought some supplies," her father said, patting his pockets. "Not even a dose of aspirin."

Aunt Tiny was cutting a loaf of bread. Eddie was standing next to her looking worried.

"I have some bandages and aspirin somewhere," Aunt Tiny said, reaching for the honey pot.

"I'm alright," Gwen murmured in between mouthfuls of tea. "Just so tired."

"You need energy," her father said.

"Here, this might help." Aunt Tiny put a slice of buttered bread smeared with honey in front of her. "It's days since you ate anything."

Gwen picked it up in her fingertips. Everyone was watching her. Her aunt clicked her fingers as if just remembering something.

"I'll be back in a little while," she said, wiping her hands on her apron and going out of the kitchen door. "Help yourselves to more tea."

"I should go too. My mum will want to know you are safe," Eddie said, not looking at Gwen. "Maybe see you later."

Gwen's father got up from his chair and stopped Eddie in the doorway.

"I want to thank you for helping to find our Gwen," he said, holding out his hand.

Eddie shook it awkwardly.

"She found herself really," he said. "Didn't need me."

Gwen shook her head, but couldn't say anything because her mouth was full of bread and honey.

"See you," Eddie called, already halfway across the yard.

Her father watched him go then turned around, a small smile playing on his lips.

"Seems a nice lad."

Gwen took a sip of tea to hide her face.

"Gwen, where have you been?" her mother said. "Your poor aunt has been frantic for you. And we –" She looked up at Alfred and sniffed hard. "Well, we thought we might have lost you too." She dug in the pocket of her suit and took out a fresh hankie. Gwen looked into her swollen, bloodshot eyes.

"I'm sorry. I went looking for Boo. He must have fallen down part of the cliff in the quarry in the dark. He landed on a narrow ledge." Gwen looked down at her plate. "I tried to lift him out, and then I fell down too. We were stuck on this ledge next to some ravens' nests, and we couldn't go anywhere. Then

Eddie found us this morning and pulled us up. I had to cling on to a long branch. That's why my hands are so scratched."

She didn't dare look up. It sounded a weak and unlikely story to her, but her parents would probably send her to the mad house if she said what really happened.

Perhaps she would be able to tell them one day.

"You should have gone to get help to rescue the dog from the cliff," her mother was saying. "You could have fallen to your death!"

"I know. It was stupid of me," Gwen said quietly. "I won't do anything like it ever again." She crossed her legs because her fingers were too sore to move.

She looked up and caught her mother and father exchanging glances.

"Well, we certainly owe that lad more than a handshake," her father said. "I'll go and smoke a pipe and think about how to repay him." He winked at Gwen and went out into the yard.

His hands still shook and his hair was grey, but he was looking better than he had for a long time.

Gwen's mother slumped a little in her chair and reached out for her tea.

"I think I'll have to have a lie down," she said. "I didn't sleep a wink last night, and we were both up at five a.m. to get here."

"I'm sorry, Mummy," Gwen said.

"No darling, I'm not cross with you. I'm so glad you are safe." She smiled a rare, fully contented smile. "Did Daddy tell you he has been discharged?"

Gwen nodded.

Her mother looked out of the window.

"I think the worst is over," she whispered.

But there was still a war, still planes dropping bombs on their factories and homes.

"Mummy, can you and Daddy come and stay here with Aunt Tiny and me?" Gwen asked.

Her mother put her teacup down carefully.

"Well, we can stay for a night or two," she said. "I've been given three days off work."

"But I mean –"

"I know darling. You want us to stay here with you for the rest of the war." Her mother sighed and stretched her arms above her head. "It would be lovely, but we just can't do that. I have to work for the arms factory. The soldiers at the Front are relying on us. And your father must work in Birmingham, treating all the people with their illnesses and wounds. They need him there." She got up from the table and went to the window.

"But it is beautiful here, and so safe. And you have a chance to be with animals, which you always wanted." She turned around and looked at Gwen. "Are you happy here? Do you mind staying?"

The nighttime crawl into the elves' green-lit realm flashed before Gwen's eyes. Safe was not the word she would use, but now that they had a pact it should be different.

"Yes, Mummy. I'm happy here."

"Oh good," her mother sighed. "I thought you and Aunt Tiny would get on."

"Speak of the devil," Aunt Tiny said, coming into the kitchen.

Gwen's father was behind her, tapping his pipe against the doorframe. She was carrying one of the stands from her studio, but this one wasn't hidden by wet muslin. It was covered in a bright blue silk scarf.

"Come into the parlour. I have something to show you."

They followed her into the shadowy room. Aunt Tiny put the stand down in the middle of the carpet and turned around.

"Lil, can you open the curtains?"

Light flooded in, showing swirls of dust, the shawls on the chairs and the rich brown of the polished piano. Aunt Tiny pushed the hair out of her face. For the first time in Gwen's memory, she looked shy.

"I hope you don't mind. I felt I just had to make it. It's for you," she said, looking at her sister. "I had it cast last week."

Gwen's mother had become very still. Her hands were gripping each other.

Aunt Tiny lifted the silk away.

It was Hugh.

Hugh as Gwen remembered him from the summer before he died. He looked happy. His mouth was open, about to call out, as if he'd seen something wonderful. His hair was flying around his face as it had when they went to the seaside. His eyes were wide.

Gwen put her hand out to trace the waves of his hair. They looked so light, so real.

Behind Gwen, her mother was crying, and her father too. They were holding each other, but Gwen just wanted to hold her brother. Not noticing that they were sore, she ran her hands over his nose and mouth. She looked over at her aunt.

Aunt Tiny was wiping her eyes with a handkerchief, but she was also watching Gwen.

"Do you like it darling?" she asked, quietly.

Gwen nodded.

"It looks just like him." She put her arms around the head of her brother and pressed the side of her face to his bronze hair. It was cold but also very solid.

Her father put his hand on her shoulder.

"Let us have a look," he said softly. "Stand next to him."

Gwen stood next to Hugh's portrait, her hand on the start of his chest where the sculpture ended, staring back at her mother and father.

They looked at the children side by side for a moment, and then pulled Aunt Tiny and Gwen and the statue together into an embrace that went on for a very long time.

I am indebted to:

Traditions, Superstitions, and Folklore by Charles Hardwick, 1872, for folklore information and for various passages quoted in the story.

The popular music hall song 'Daddy Wouldn't Buy Me a Bow-wow' written in 1892 by Joseph Tabrar, found on www.mfiles.co.uk

Also to the Twitter account 'Hookland' @HooklandGuide for the following fictional quote:

> *"They call the faery 'Greencoats' at Ravenshaw, for locals claim that this is the garb they are always seen wearing when encountered thereabouts."* Rev. H R Fade, 1898

And to Anna Streetly, who created the exquisite illustrations for the cover and interior – Mike Ashton for the striking cover design – Stuart Davies for Shropshire dialect/word advice – and Ann Mason for her generous attention and sharp eye.

My thanks to Caroline Lawrence, Anne Marie Lagram, Honor Bleackley, Amelie Maynard, Sarah Lamsdale, Sarah Ibberson, Susie Stapleton, Lucy Armstrong-Blair, Ted Eames, Kate and Charlie Smith, Jonathan Davidson, Maeve Clarke, William Gallagher, Jane Roberts, Liz Hyder, Michael, Braw, Alex and Jill Innes who all kindly read and commented on the text and provided so much moral support.

Finally –thanks to all my family for their loving help, especially John who listened and commented as each chapter was written.